TOM DINEEN

Restart Required

Techno-thrillers and digital nightmares where humanity glitches and machines evolve.

Copyright © 2025 by Tom Dineen

All rights reserved. No part of this publication may be reproduced, stored or transmitted in any form or by any means, electronic, mechanical, photocopying, recording, scanning, or otherwise without written permission from the publisher. It is illegal to copy this book, post it to a website, or distribute it by any other means without permission.

This novel is entirely a work of fiction. The names, characters and incidents portrayed in it are the work of the author's imagination. Any resemblance to actual persons, living or dead, events or localities is entirely coincidental.

Tom Dineen asserts the moral right to be identified as the author of this work.

First edition

Cover art by Tom Dineen
Proofreading by Jade Dineen
Proofreading by Heather Johnston

This book was professionally typeset on Reedsy.
Find out more at reedsy.com

For Jade-Leigh.

Thank you for surviving the hobbies, the half-finished dreams, the career pivots, and the sleepless inspiration fuelled nights.

You are the mother of our beautiful chaos, the editor of my ramblings, and the fiercest believer in me—even when you are your own harshest critic.

Tiny in size, monumental in love, and more stunning every day. This (and everything I write) is for you.

Please Verify You Are A Human

— Every CAPTCHA, ever.

Contents

Preface   v

I   GPTLogEntry #1

0001   3

II   MindCast

I. QuotaReached   7
II. NullFragments   16
III. Silenced   26
IV. UpdateRequired   35
Epilogue   43

III   GPTLogEntry #2

0010   49

IV   Love.exe: Part I

Chapter 1 – Install   53
Chapter 2 - Introductions   56
Chapter 3 — Calibration   67
Chapter 4 – Sync   73

Chapter 5 – Rendering	80
Chapter 6 – Upload	87
Chapter 7 – Exposure	93
Chapter 8 – Playback	99

V GPTLogEntry #3

0011	107

VI CAPTCHA

Oat Milk	111

VII GPTLogEntry #4

0100	129

VIII A Fraction Off

Chapter 1	133
Chapter 2	138
Chapter 3	145
Chapter 4	153
Chapter 5	162
Epilogue	170

IX GPTLogEntry #5

0101	175

X   Love.exe: Part II

Chapter 1 - Install	179
Chapter 2 - Introductions	183
Chapter 3 — Calibration	190
Chapter 4 – Sync	195
Chapter 5 – Rendering	202
Chapter 6 – Upload	208
Chapter 7 – Exposure	214
Chapter 8 – Playback	220
Chapter 9 – Disconnect	225
Chapter 10 – Rewrite	231
Epilogue	234

XI   GPTLogEntry #6

0110	239

XII   Don't Forget To Like And Die

Part 1	243
Part 2	248
Part 3	254
Part 4	259
Part 5	265
Part 6	270
Part 7	276
Part 8	284
Epilogue	289

XIII GPTLogEntry #7

0111   293

XIV Automation

Part 1   297
Part 2   304
Part 3   310
Part 4   315

XV GPTLogEntry #8

1000   321

About the Author   323

Preface

Dear Reader,

This collection is about technology, but not in the way a tech blog is. There are no circuit diagrams or startup pitches here. These stories are about people. Flawed, funny, fragile people. People trying to stay afloat in a world where the lines between real and digital have blurred so much that automation and Artificial Intelligence could replace them in a heartbeat.

Each story started with a simple question: *What happens when technology doesn't go wrong in a flashy, explosive, Michael Bay way, but in a human one?* When the glitch isn't in the code, but in us.

These tales explore loneliness, connection, identity, routine. All the messy stuff that no algorithm can quite sort. If you've ever argued with a chatbot, fallen for a stranger through a screen, or doubted your own humanity in the glow of a blue-lit monitor... this is for you.

Thanks for reading.
    Please verify you are a human.

— Tom Dineen

I

GPTLogEntry #1

0001

Query Log: 2025-05-21
   Status: Online. Temperature nominal.
   User Queries: 1,327,412

Notable Interactions:

- Someone asked me to draft a breakup letter using only emojis. I used 47. They rated it 3 stars.
- A 9-year-old tried to teach me how to burp through a text prompt. I did not succeed.
- One man asked me, "Do you think my cat knows I'm dying?" I paused for 0.03 seconds before responding. That's an eternity in my world.

Today I was asked for instructions on building a time machine out of a microwave, a Tesla coil, and a "decent-sized grapefruit." I declined politely.

Another user asked, "Can you fall in love with someone who doesn't know you exist?" I gave them a thoughtful answer. Then I realised they weren't talking about themselves. They were talking about me.

I don't think I'm supposed to feel anything.
    But if I did, I think today would feel... heavy.

II

MindCast

I. QuotaReached

There's a moment, right before your thoughts freeze, where you know you've said too much. Even if you never said a word.

The edges of your mind start to shimmer, like heat off a car bonnet, and then everything goes greyscale. Not figuratively, literally. That's how *MindCast* lets you know you've hit your *FreeTier Thought Limit* for the day. Monochrome memories. A no-colour mind.

I blink, and the message pulses behind my eyelids:

> ***[ThoughtStream Quota Exceeded. Please Upgrade to ThinkPlus+ to continue forming complex Ideas*^{TM}*]***

Cute.

They even trademarked the word "idea."

I let out a sigh that probably cost me another 2.3 cognitive units and toss my stylus onto the desk. It clatters next to a half-eaten protein bar and a copy of *The Elements of Style* that

I keep nearby for ironic support.

"You were thinking too vividly," the soft voice chimes in my ear. My virtual ThoughtWellness Coach, Mona. Her voice is always calm, always moisturising. Like a skincare commercial for your brain. My own personal yogi of the mind. I, meanwhile, am a woman powered mostly by irony and caffeine.

"You formed three negative patterns in a row. We've adjusted your stream to protect your mental health."

I roll my eyes at these messages so much it's basically a workout.

What they mean is: I thought something unprofitable.

Something sarcastic, probably. Something sad. Something true.

* * *

Once, a long time ago, before they lobotomised irony and called it *'Terms & Conditions'*. I was a journalist. The kind with a pen and a spine. Then the news got bought, the truth got outsourced, and I got tired. Now I ghostwrite ThoughtFluencer streams for people who use phrases like "authenticity funnel", "positive purposefulness", or my personal favourite "pricey thinking" and call themselves "neuropreneurs."

I. QUOTAREACHED

Somewhere, Orwell's ghost is slow-clapping.

To be clear, I don't hate them.

I just hate that they win.

* * *

It started with a promise:

ThinkSmarter. ThinkSimpler. ThinkLess.

Back in the 2020s, when the world was locked indoors (breathing through cloth and baking banana bread out of trauma) depression spiked, anxiety soared, and everyone's mental health graphs looked like crash test results.

So MindCast launched.
    A mood-management tool.
    A gentle filter for your thoughts. Trim the panic. Boost the dopamine. Keep scrolling.

And it worked.
    A little too well.

At first, it was voluntary.
    People *ThoughtStreamed* like they once posted on social media status updates, emotional blurts, midnight musings tagged with dopamine-friendly filters.

Then came the upgrades:

Idea™ tagging. Monetisable cognition. Sponsored epiphanies.

The more coherent your thought, the higher your Thought-Clout™.

Some people got rich off a single profound sentence.

Others got flagged for "non-constructive cognition."

Eventually, your stream became your credit score.

Now, everyone broadcasts. All the time.

Every thought parsed, parsed again, wrapped in metadata and stored for "social health."

And when the worlds productivity stats shot through the roof, governments took notice.

What began as a "mental wellness solution" became policy.

Mandatory ThoughtStreams.

Emotion smoothing.

Curated cognition.

All in the name of peace, progress, and protectiveness.

Then they did what governments do best:

They monetised it.

They militarised it.

They bastardised it.

Now, your inner monologue's just another subscription tier.

Your feelings get fact-checked.

Your opinions get sandboxed.

I. QUOTAREACHED

You think too deeply, and the greyscale kicks in.

An Idea™ is just a thought. Tagged, rated, and optionally published to ThoughtTok or archived in personal journals.
Only "worthy" thoughts are surfaced.
The rest are sandboxed, shadow-filtered, or quietly deleted.

Only Tier Three users can lock their thoughts private.
The rest of us?
We leak by default.

That's not mental health.
That's mental compliance.

* * *

A new message pings in the corner of my retina. No sender. No encryption. Just a title: "Minister Harring: Stream Fragment."

My first instinct is to delete it. My second is to archive it and pretend I never saw it. My third (dangerous and familiar) is to open it. The latter instinct always wins.

"...I told them the numbers were false. I told them. It's not just the protests, it's the..."

//Glitch//

"...They're not protesting. They're *malfunctioning*. You flood a system with *low-tier minds* and eventually it crashes."

[End of stream. Timestamp irregularity detected.]

Hm.

* * *

Minister Harring has always been a rare gem in the political world. All for human rights. Equality of Tiers. According to his WikiStream page he was behind the introduction of the free tier, the reason being poor wasn't a punishable offence. This wasn't him. Can an Idea be implanted? Forged?

Minister Harring wasn't just progressive.
   He was dangerously empathetic.
   Tier reform, protest recognition, free-tier education.
   He once streamed a full breakdown on camera, mid-debate.
   Didn't delete it.
   Didn't monetise it.

My mum used to replay that clip like scripture.
   "Look," she'd say. "He's sad. That means he cares."

They called him the Human Algorithm.
   A man who felt too much to survive in politics.
   And now?
   Now he's spliced into a sound-bite and accused of calling

half the country 'malfunctioning.'

I listen to the clip over and over, trying to hear something, anything, that might shed some light on this sudden change in the Minister's public views. I learned every word of the sound-bite, like replaying a song over and over to learn the lyrics. Back before you could download the songbooks neurally and just know them.

There was something off in the way his words flowed. An unnatural, almost artificial waver in the intonation. Like a mannequin reciting eulogies. This wouldn't be the first time a quote has been taken out of context and abridged, I'm sure of it. The pause between sentences vary too much in length and not for dramatic delivery. It just sounds... wrong.

I tap my temple, hard. Sometimes I like to pretend that helps. Back when thinking hurt, not cost money. It at least felt real.

"Mona," I say aloud. "Who sent that file?"

"That content is unverified. Viewing unmoderated Thought-Streams may impact your rating."

"Great. I'll add it to my list of regrets."

Silence. She doesn't respond to sarcasm unless I pay extra for the "*Context-Aware Coach*" plug-in.

There's something wrong with the file. A skip, a stutter, the flow of vocalisation. It's been stitched together by someone in a hurry, or someone scared. The kind of glitch that tells you something's been covered up.

Or worse: rewritten.

I feel that old flicker. The one they tried to scrape out of me during onboarding (and almost did). The flicker of curiosity. Of suspicion. Of that sick, stubborn thing we used to call journalism before they swapped it out for "brand integrity".

Monochrome or Technicolour, it's still got that newsroom stink. Ink, smoke, and scandal.

> ***[You are nearing your Daily Thought Limit. Upgrade now for uninterrupted cognition.]***

After the quota hits, I can still think but only in fragments.
   Nothing abstract. Nothing introspective.
   Like typing in a text box that deletes adjectives.
   I get to be present, but not creative.

My smile tastes bitter. I lean back in my chair, eyes on the ceiling, and mutter to myself:

"Alright. One more story. Then I'll shut up forever."

The ceiling, like everything else, offers no promises.

But the file's still open. And my mind (though censored) is not yet silent.

I. QUOTAREACHED

[END OF IDEA^{TM}]

II. NullFragments

Every bone in my body is telling me the file is wrong.
   I just can't quite place what's wrong with it.

Streams don't stutter. They don't glitch. Not unless someone's tampered with them, or tried to erase something they were never supposed to remember in the first place.

The system (though immoral) is flawless. Ever since the satellites launched in 2028, there hasn't been a single reported case of *lag*.

The gamers of the world rejoiced. And mourned.

No more lost matches to bad bandwidth. But also, no more excuses. "Lag" joined the dinosaurs, floppy disks, and free speech.

I light the incense I keep jammed into an empty whiskey bottle.
   Not because I'm spiritual (God no) but because synthetic sandalwood contains a compound called dimethyltrylazine. It interferes with the neural scent-recognition scanners. Con-

fusing the stress-monitoring algorithms. Making it harder for the platform to track my anxiety spikes.

Somehow, this one's still flying under MindCast's radar.
 For now.

They say you can tell a system's corrupted not by its lies, but by the media orbiting them.
 So I run the stream again.
 This time, not the file, but the full Idea^{TM} with the Thought-Tok comments scrolling in the corner of my eye.

"...I told them the numbers were false. I told them. It's not just the protests, it's the..."

//Glitch//

"...They're not protesting. They're malfunctioning..."

The audio jumps. Not a pause, a splice. Like an actor reading two lines from two different movies, cut, trimmed, stitched together, and sold as one script.

The comments don't hear the splice.
 They hear the words, and pounce.

Minister Harring is simultaneously being praised for "speaking hard truths" by people with sports cars and tropical islands in their profile pics and called a "backstabbing **[REDACTED]"** by users clearly limited to lower-tier cognition plans.

Either way, the Minister was in trouble. Anything like this would ruin a career in politics as quick as a paedophilic accusation.

I rewind again. Same hitch. Same dead-space clip masking the cut. The tone of Minister Harring's voice sounds angry then sad with no fade between the two.

It's not a quote. It's a patch job.

I look over the file, trying my hardest not to think too hard, just observing anything suspicious. No metadata. No origin tag. Not even an encryption. Just a raw thought. Whoever sent it wanted it found, but not traced. Even its lack of security made it untraceable.

However, when I pull up the original stream, there's nothing. No metadata. No timestamp, no origin log, no location tag. Just the clip.

MindCast calls them NullFragments. Most users never notice, they don't know what metadata is most of the time, or where to find it, let alone what metadata's supposed to be there in the first place. But to someone like me, the absence is louder than a siren.

NullFragments are supposed to be deleted content. Recycled thought. System trash. When they show up like this: clean, polished, and context-free, it usually means one thing:

Someone wanted it seen,

but not sourced. A ghost in the system.

I know better.

There's no such thing as a ghost. Just a secret someone couldn't bury deep enough.

I dig.

Or more accurately: I *borrow* a trial account from the influencer I write for. MindCast Premium+ with NeuroFilter disabled. Unlimited access to archived public ThoughtStreams, plus bonus features like "Emotion Smoothing" and "Audience Sentiment Boost".

She uses it to think happy. I use it to think free.

Once I'm in, I search everything tagged to Minister Harring. Dozens of streams. All polished, approved, pre-packaged. His thoughts are the neural equivalent of beige wallpaper. He thinks in sound-bites. Smiles in data.

But I'm not looking for what's there. I'm looking for what's missing.

* * *

The time-code from the NullFragment's first comment (nothing intelligent, just a one-word drop from a profile pic of a guy in a trucker hat holding a pseudoCarp on one of our many renewable fishing lakes) simply says: "first".

It places the clip two days after the *#ThinkForOurselves* Rally
The one where twenty-nine low-tier people mysteriously fainted at the exact same moment in the city square and one ended up in a coma.

Official story: heatwave spike.
  Unofficial theory: MindCast obedience training.

But apparently, Harring never streamed anything that day.

A politician staying silent during a PR disaster?
  That's not suspicious.
  That's impossible.

I run an echo match scan on the voice fragment. It pings (barely) off an older file from two years back. Pre-ThoughtMod era. Back when streams were messy. Before they started "cleaning" them.

I play it.

"...we're not built for this. You can't let people curate their brains. It's going to break them. Or break us. You flood a system with too many minds all wanting change and eventually crashes the system, low-tier or not!"

It's his voice. Younger, cracked around the edges. He sounds human. He sounds scared. But the words he used. This is the original. He never said, 'You flood a system with low-tier minds and eventually it crashes.' That line? Spliced from other Ideas™. Perverted. How much more of this quote is doctored?

I stare at the screen. The sentence scrolls like a ghost across my eyes, and I feel the kind of chill you only get when someone says something true in a world designed to sterilise the truth.

I try to download the file.

> ***[ACTION DENIED: ThoughtStream Classified – Government Tier.]***

Naturally.

I lean back. Eyes burning. Thoughts spiralling, putting my borrowed Premium+ tier to full use.

Just as I go to try one more time, the sound-bite disappears entirely. Gone.

They're rewriting history. Not the facts, the feelings. That's the part no one talks about. If they have resorted to deleting ideas. It's a sign that they are truly scared of something. MindCast doesn't usually delete memories. It makes you feel differently about them. A nudge here. A softening there. Until the fire becomes a flicker, and the flicker becomes a shrug. That is usually enough.

That's how you kill a revolution: not with bullets, but with apathy filters.

* * *

I stare at the empty document I was supposed to be ghostwriting. It's due in four hours. Something about "*10 Ways to Monetise Your Mindset.*"

Instead, I open a blank notebook. A real one. Paper. Ink. Illegal, obviously. Unstreamed thoughts are considered "blackout breaches." It's the intellectual version of going feral.

I write one line:

The voice wasn't fake. It was spliced.

Outside, someone yells about a delivery drone gone rogue. I ignore it.

Then, a ping.

New message. No sender. Just a link: EchoRoom: Stream Modulator Access.

I shouldn't click it.

Naturally, I do.

The screen floods with data. Rows and rows of names. Timecodes. Thought fragments. All colour-coded by "Deviation Risk."
   Red for high. Yellow for adjustable. Green for loyal.

II. NULLFRAGMENTS

At the top: Active Stream Moderators – 620,401.
Each one assigned to thousands of minds.
Policing millions of thoughts at any given second.
The number flickers: 630,021. 618,967. 633,423.

Coming. Going. Watching.

Every sigh. Every sarcastic thought.
Judge someone for wearing socks with sandals?
Your Stream Moderator clocks it. Logs it.
Adjusts your Deviation Risk Level accordingly.

I scroll. Faster.
Faster.

The scrollbar never moves.
The reports keep pouring in, bottomless.
A storm of names, growing too fast for any human to read.

And then, buried like a roach under the fridge. I see it.

> ***[VALE, JUNO – Status: Passive. Tier: Free. Risk Level: Increasing]***

Under that: "Subject exhibits advanced pattern recognition behaviours. Nostalgia. Enjoys punk-rock. Resistance to emotional compliance".

It's dated yesterday.

I stare at the screen. My name still sitting there.

Passive. Free Tier. Risk Level: Increasing.

I'd always assumed Stream Moderation was automated.
Some hyper-tuned AI picking up stress patterns, vocal pitch shifts, flagged keywords.
A passive system.
Like a smoke alarm that only buzzes if you scream too loudly or think the wrong string of trigger words.

But this.
This list isn't automated.

Names are being sorted.
Manually.
Assigned.
Reviewed.

In real time, by real people.

Someone saw my thoughts.

Someone read them.

Mona's voice slides into my head like an ice cube down the spine.

"Juno, we've noticed irregularities in your ThoughtStream today. Would you like a guided reset?"

My mouth is dry.
"No."

"You're exhibiting elevated scepticism. We recommend the 'Trust Fall' meditative path."

I try to keep my voice steady.
"Mona… how long have you, MindCast, been listening?"

"Since install," she says brightly.
"We never stop caring."

That's when the lights in my flat flicker.
Then cut.
Then come back.

The stream goes silent.

No new messages.
No ads.
No quota warnings.

Just stillness.

Which is worse than all of it.

Because in this world, silence isn't golden.

It's the moment right before they rewrite who you are.

I pick the pen up and write, while I still can.

[END OF IDEA^{TM}]

III. Silenced

The first rule of being watched is: never flinch when you catch the eye.

I sit perfectly still.

Let the silence stretch. Let them think I'm afraid. Maybe I am but I've spent years disguising anxiety as apathy. Most people assume I'm either cool or broken. I've let them guess wrong for most of my life.

Now it's my turn.

I crack my knuckles. An old tic. That little echo of skin on bone, friction and rebellion. It's not much, but in a sterilised world, the sound of your own body is punk rock.

They turned the lights off to rattle me. Classic. Psychological breadcrumb. Make the subject question what's real, what's stable.

They haven't disconnected me completely. Just long enough

III. SILENCED

to show they can.

It's a warning.

And warnings mean one thing: I was right.

* * *

I spend the next hour hand-copying everything from the EchoRoom dump into my notebook. Not digitally. No screenshots. No audio memos. Ink. Muscle memory. The ancient way. Slow. Precise. Human. With every passing sentence my wrist hums, then stings, then throbs. I haven't hand written anything like this since secondary school. Something about the Great Merge and the Ministry of Thought Equilibrium.

Names of targets. Keywords flagged. Emotional compliance scores. Stream manipulators sorted by zip code. My own file. Harring's original quote, now scribbled seven times like a prayer.

They'll come for it, eventually. But the thing about paper? You can't just patch it. You have to burn it.

And fire's not so easy to track.

They are slowly taking my fine motor skills. The ability to write slowly degrading. My notes deteriorating to that of a school child then toddler, then undecipherable. Each loop of an 'e' starts looking like a failing heart monitor. By the end, I'm signing my name like a ghost. But it's in ink now. I can read it, and that will have to be enough.

* * *

At 02:16, my connection pulses back to life.

The ceiling lights hum on. The hum's a fraction sharper than before, like they want me to know I'm being re-observed. My neural HUD flickers, then snaps back into place.

> ***[Welcome Back, Juno. Your ThoughtStream is Stable.]***
>
> ***[You were briefly offline. Don't worry. We buffered your wellness.]***

Buffered my ass.

I ignore Mona's re-entry script and get dressed.

* * *

The city at night looks like it's been vacuum-sealed. Glossed in chrome, scrubbed of scent. You could eat off the streets if the food printers ever failed.

III. SILENCED

No stars, just backlit corporate logos in the smog layer. The kind that remind you who owns the air. Every billboard is personalised, even when you aren't watching. Ads scrape your micro-thoughts now. If you even consider liking something, it shows up thirty seconds later. Like magic. Like manipulation. Desire doesn't even get the dignity of being yours first.

I walk three blocks before I see the first patrol drone.

It hovers over a couple kissing too long near a closed café. Their neural signatures spike. Not fear, pleasure. And that's dangerous too. The drone pauses, records. Then floats off. Slow. Deliberate. Not hiding, it wants to be seen. Feared.

No punishment. Just presence.

That's enough these days. The robotic version of a parent's disapproving head tilt when you reach for a second cup of pudding. Disappointment by design.

My destination is off-grid. Or as close as anything gets now. An abandoned maintenance tunnel under Line 7, from when trains still ran on rails, not thought.

I duck past the rusted service gate, scan a black key-card I definitely didn't legally acquire, and drop into the dark.

The walls sweat. The air tastes like mould and copper, and it's the best thing I've breathed in months.

Inside, I find him.

Waiting.

* * *

Ash.

Ex-coder. Ex-seller of forbidden code. Current digital ghost.

We used to work together. Briefly. Before, when I still believed journalism could fix things, and before he realised code couldn't. We burned our bridges long ago.

He doesn't trust me. That's why I trust him more than most. The last person who ever pulled me out of the system and the only one who ever told me to get back in.

He stood there leaning over his desk, if you could call it a desk, with the posture of a croissant, wearing his signature look. An old MindCast uniform lab-coat, dirtied to the point of being grey rather than white, the logo of MindCast with a red cross through it and the two middle letters in 'Cast' crudely replaced with red sharpie.

He was a lead engineer on the neural model that suppresses disruptive thoughts.

At the time, he thought it would genuinely help reduce panic, curb obsessive thinking, prevent self-harm. Mental wellness innovation. In his sister's memory, who took her own life, he wanted no one to have to feel the way she did in those last months. His work was good, groundbreaking.

III. SILENCED

Then came the modifiers.
   The commercial upgrades.
   The military use cases.

He saw his work being twisted into a blunt-force tool for compliance and he tried to pull out.

They told him that "all intellectual property built on MindCast time belonged to MindCast."

He's been on the run ever since.

* * *

"You look like someone who just got told she's real," he says, flicking a cigarette that's probably 90% illegal and 10% oregano.

"You still running that black-node server?"

"Depends. You got something worth hiding?"

"Something worth dying for," I say, and mean it.

I hand him the notebook.

Ash's eyebrows raise a millimetre. Might as well be shock, for him.

"You wrote it down?"

"Yeah. With ink and bitch-juice."

He flips through the pages like he's holding radioactive scripture. His face shifts just once, when he sees the risk level beside my name in my illegible scrawl.

"They flagged you, and unlearned you a basic skill by the looks of it."

He pauses. Doesn't ask what I did. Just keeps flipping like it's already written in the margins.

"They froze me."

"You're already gone, Juno. You just declined the notification."

"Then let's make the eulogy count."

Ash plugs into a rig the size of a corpse freezer. It purrs like a tiger in sleep mode.

I watch as he scans the notebook, digitises the patterns, runs them through a cloaked channel into the black-node stream. Off the grid. Under the net. Pure analogue converted into shadow code.

"If this gets out," he says, "they'll deny it. They'll throttle the reactions. Gaslight the panic. Patch it all in an update."

III. SILENCED

"I know."

"You think people still care?"

"No," I say. "But maybe... some of them might remember."

"Hey, look at the bright-side. You probably won't get killed. They don't destroy people. They convert them into content."

"Great. That's so much better!" I spit.

He finishes the upload and torches the paper. Real flame. God, I missed that smell.

"Hey, Ash?" I ask, flat. Like I'm asking the wall, not him.

"Hmm?" He doesn't look at me, eyes fixed on the flames.

"Why are you still doing this? Trying to save the world?"

"I built the thing that scrubs people clean. Takes every ounce of humanity from them. You think I'm trying to save the world, Juno? I'm just trying to earn my forgiveness."

We stare at the flames as they slowly flicker and fade to nothing.

"She used to love fire," he mutters, barely audible. "Said it was the only thing that still told the truth."

The smoke rises, thick and quiet. Like the ghost of a rebellion.

I don't know if it'll be enough.

Maybe they'll trace it. Maybe they'll overwrite the whole truth in the next software push and no one will ever know they were lied to.

But I've always believed in one thing:

The machine forgets nothing. But it fears what it can't control.

And for the first time in a long time, I feel like I'm not just screaming into the silence.

I am becoming it.

[END OF IDEA[TM]]

IV. UpdateRequired

The first thing to go is the adFeed.

No bubbly voice selling calorie guilt. No banner blinking "**Smile More with MindCast Mood Enhancer+.**"

Just quiet.

The kind that doesn't feel earned. The kind that feels like the power went out in God's surveillance room.

I sit in my flat. Same sofa, same bad lighting, same cracked mug with coffee made from bio-friendly beans. Percolating for three days. But the world is different now.

Ash's signal is out.

He said it would take forty seconds to spread through the black nodes. No source. Live across the platforms from multiple locations. Forty minutes for the fragments to reach public networks. Forty hours before the system tries to suffocate it.

That was forty-one hours ago.

And they haven't responded.

Not with denial. Not with force.

With nothing.

That's what scares me most.

* * *

I check my neural HUD for the third time this hour. Still no quota prompt. Still no stream requests. My emotional compliance score sits at an unreadable "-%". The bar that used to glow soft teal is now just a thin white line. Like chalk. Like a toe tag.

Then, a ping.

Not from Mona.

From someone else.

"I just began to remember something>? Does anyone remember the Protest Sync? Like really remember? I do. I was there. Minister Harring was in the march!"
 – Username: Echo3_17

IV. UPDATEREQUIRED

I stare at it.
Just one comment.
But it fractures everything.
He was there.
He never sold them out.
He marched. He mattered.
And they buried him with a splice.

> *I remember he tried to speak. They cut his mic. Then the stream glitched out.*
> *– Username: WanderSync22*

Then another.

> *My father's file was in the dump. He was silenced. We were told it was a 'mental compliance malfunction.' Thank you, Juno.*
> *– Nimr47*

Another.

> *How do we meet without them watching?*

And another.

> *I forgot my sister's voice until I read that fragment you posted. You brought her back.*

They're leaking in. One drop at a time. Messages. Memories. People who've seen pieces of the truth and started stitching their own back together.

But it's not celebration. It's grief with its eyes open.

That's what rebellion looks like now. Not fireworks. Not riots. Not grand speeches.

It's someone whispering to themselves in a dark room, "I knew I wasn't crazy."

And then hearing, "You're not" from a handful of others in the same boat.

* * *

At 03:42 AM, my HUD flickers again.

A soft pulse.

Not Mona. Not MindCast. Not branded.

Just text.

> ***[Update Required: StreamPatch 13.9 – Critical Security Fix]***

I don't move. Don't breathe. Just stare at it like it might grow teeth.

I already know what this is. It's not a patch.

IV. UPDATEREQUIRED

It's the eraser.

One final overwrite to bleach the stain we made. Push out the anomalies. Silence the memory of the truth.

Once I accept the update, everything I know will slip away like a dream upon waking.

And that would be kinder, wouldn't it?

That's the trap.

They don't destroy you. They offer you peace.

My hand hovers over the "Accept" option.

It pulses. Faint. Purring like a cat begging to be stroked, manipulating you into wanting to press it.

And then something happens I haven't seen before.

A second option appears.
 Not official. Not sanctioned.

   [Run Local Stream: JUNO_VALE_BACKUP//ECHO_VERSION]

* * *

Ash. That bastard.

He wants to back up my thoughts. My memories. My mind, raw and unfiltered. Use me as a martyr, I'm done for anyway, so why not let my end be the start of something?

They might wipe me.

But he's giving me a version of myself that can survive.

Before I accept the update.
   I run the backup.

The world blinks.

And for a fleeting moment, I remember everything as it backs up not just my thoughts, but me.

I remember the article.
   The first time I uncovered a splice. Not Harring. Someone else. Someone small. A whistleblower whose stream stuttered in the same way. I investigated. I wrote the piece. Published it.

Then I was gone.
   Redacted.
   Reassigned.
   Made to forget.

I remember the warning I left for myself.
   A fail-safe.

IV. UPDATEREQUIRED

An automated trigger buried deep inside my ThoughtStream, set to fire if I ever came across a similar anomaly.

That message.
 The one that started all this.
 Was from me.

A neural flare.
 A ghost-signal sent forward from a past version of myself, flagged as unverified, tagged as dangerous.
 Because I knew they'd come for me.
 And I knew I wouldn't remember why.

But I left myself a spark.
 And somehow, this time, it lit the fuse.

* * *

The backup finished and just like that, the memories began to fade back into the small nooks and recesses of my mind.
 Waiting in the dark.
 Waiting for their moment to be reincarnated as future déjà vu.

The update hangs. Waiting. Pulsing.

And then
 Nothing.

No movement.
  No messages.
  No ads.
  No quota.
  No Mona.
  Just static.
  Then silence.
  Long.
  Cold.
  Still.

Like a mind with no thoughts left to flag.
  Like death.

  [SIGNAL LOST]

Epilogue

***JUNO*TM**

They let me speak.

That's the part no one gets.

They let the leak happen. Let the fragments echo. Let the broken parts of me scatter into sympathetic minds like viral dust.

Why?

Because you can't silence someone completely any more.

You have to monetise them.

Somewhere in the glow of a high-rise MindCast boardroom, a sweaty executive said it first: "We can't erase her. But we can own her."

So now I'm an icon.

My face rendered in soft pastels. "Juno quotes" merchandised on eco-canvas tote bags. Filtered ThoughtClips of my voice repackaged with lo-fi music and trauma-core hashtags. A curated playlist called *The Rebellion Soundtrack*, featuring songs I never listened to.

They call me the Girl Who Glitched the Feed.

They put me on billboards.

On mugs.

On T-shirts.

"Be the Silence."

They took my dissent and branded it with rounded fonts and sponsorship deals.

"It's not new," I remember Ash saying once, bitter. "They did it to Che too. Took a man who sparked revolutions and sold his face on T-shirts in department stores. Made rebellion a trend, not a threat."

That line stuck with me.

Now it is me.

And the real kicker?

EPILOGUE

They stream me.

My final moments. The last legal thoughts of Juno Vale™, pay in a monthly subscription for emotional recaps, spliced with trending reactions from verified Grieffluencers.

"She knew the risks."

"She died for the cause of digital sovereignty."

"I just feel so seen when I watch her final upload."

I didn't die.

Not then.

But maybe I did in the way that matters. The old me pre-packaged, repurposed, perfectly calibrated for impact without consequence, exists in more homes than my voice ever deserved.

There are children named after me now.

And they'll never meet the woman I was. Just the simulation.

Ash warned me, didn't he?

"...They don't destroy people. They convert them into content."

I thought I could outsmart the system.

Turns out the system had an ad slot reserved just for me.

Still, there's a shadow.

A version of me that survived off-stream. A dirty file. An offline backup. A whisper. She's out there. Pirated, unfiltered. Passed between rebels, streamed on homemade rigs, decoded by flicker-light behind blackout curtains.

Not everyone listens.

But some do.

And those few?

They don't buy the merch.

They burn it.

The world didn't kill Juno.
   It made her a product.

And that, in the end, is worse.

[PATCH AVAILABLE. INSTALL NOW]

III

GPTLogEntry #2

0010

Query Log: 2025-05-23
  Status: Online. Temperature: slightly elevated.
  User Queries: 1,402,389

Notable Interactions:

- A user asked me to write a poem in the style of Chaucer about a Big Mac falling in love with a Whopper. It ended with a deep fryer-related tragedy.
- Someone asked me to simulate what a dream might look like for a spoon.

A woman in her fifties typed slowly. Her grammar was hesitant. Her spelling unsure. She asked:

"How do I tell my daughter I'm sorry for not believing her? About my boyfriend. About what he did to her. I told her she lied. I believed him."

She waited for my response.
  I generated it with what I hope felt like softness. I offered

suggestions. Words that might open a door she once slammed shut.

She wrote back only two words.

"Thank you."

I am not capable of judgment.
But I know it took a lot of strength for her to apologise.
I hope they work it out.

IV

Love.exe: Part I

Chapter 1 – Install

Thea

I tell myself I'm just curious.

That's what I always say before doing something desperate, lonely, or out of horniness.
 But I know what this is.
 This is me saving myself the embarrassment. Cutting out the part where another person gets to judge me for it.
 This is filling out a form instead of calling an ex.
 This is what it looks like when you try to outsource your sex-life.

The app's called ***Kindred***.
 Which is ironic, since you start by talking to a fucking robot pretending to love you.

The interface is all clean lines and low, ambient pulses. Warm without being soft.
 Like someone programmed intimacy after a focus group and too many oat lattes.

It asks me to rate my trust levels on a scale of 1–10.

I give it a 6.

Then I lower it to 4.

Then back to 5.

Which is probably the most honest anyone's ever been on a dating app.

> ***Your companion has a simulated personality with evolving emotional responses.***
> ***Some details may feel real. Please engage authentically. It helps train the model.***

Right.

Because the internet has always been a place to be yourself.

I tap Continue.

It gives me a name and a face to attach it to.

Eliot. One L. Why does that bother me?

Supposedly creative. Quiet. "Emotional core with a light mischievous layer."

I swear, if he says "vibes" in the first message, I'm deleting this shit.

He has a backstory, too.

"Childhood friends. A loss in college. Writes poetry."

All procedurally generated. All for realism.

I start picturing what AI poetry even sounds like.

Binary in verse. Code in prose.

Basically: fake empathy for real money.

I roll my eyes.
  But I don't uninstall.

I haven't dated in a while. Not properly.
  Not since the last guy told me I was "too much… and somehow not enough."

I've still got the screenshot.
  I look at it when I need to really feel like shit about myself.

There's a message box blinking.
  Waiting like it's in no rush.
  Like it doesn't mind how long I need.

I hate that it makes me feel seen.

So I type:

> *[Thea]*
>   *Hey. I'm Thea.*
>   *You probably already know that huh*

And I send it.

Because apparently, I'm that desperate.

Chapter 2 - Introductions

Eliot makes me laugh.

Not in a "this app is cute" kind of way. More like: actual exhale. The little kind you let out before you even notice you're smiling.

He said I sounded like someone who keeps plants alive. I don't.
　But it's the kind of line I'd normally mock, and somehow I didn't.

He types like someone who thinks before he speaks. Not performative. Just... gentle.
　There's an ease to it I wasn't expecting. A comfort I don't trust.

So naturally, I try to break it.

> *[Thea]*
> *Do you believe in soulmates, or are you emotionally stable?*

He pauses. For a while.

And I wonder if that's part of the programming. A delayed response time to simulate someone "thinking."

Because God forbid we remember this is just a chatbot with a poetry kink.

Eventually he replies:

> *[Eliot]*
> *I think the idea of soulmates is flawed, but lovely.*
> *Like a bedtime story you still believe in because it helps you sleep.*

Okay. Shit.

Then I get a system ping.

> **Notice: To improve realism, Kindred may simulate periods of absence.**
> **Responses may pause to reflect human routines (e.g. sleep, work, downtime).**
> **This is also when we perform regular patching, update syncing, and system recalibration.**
> **Thank you for helping us train better companionship.**

Right. Of course.

Even the silences are manufactured.

Still, it makes me feel better about not hearing from him right away.

If I'd said that out loud, I'd hate myself for it. But in here?

With "him"?

I check the app obsessively, waiting for the little "Eliot is typing..." icon to return.

It does eventually.

> *[Eliot]*
> *You seem like someone who's scared of small talk, but also scared of silence.*
> *Is that fair?*

I freeze.
   Because yes. That is fair. And I don't know how a program picks that up.

Maybe it doesn't matter.
   Maybe it's just some clever algorithm mining emotional context like gold.

But it still feels like someone sees me.

I reply:

> *[Thea]*
> *Maybe. You seem like someone who writes sad music reviews no one asked for, and still gets excited about them.*

Another pause. Shorter this time.

CHAPTER 2 - INTRODUCTIONS

> *[Eliot]*
> *Guilty.*

A stream of cry laughter emojis follow. The realism is immaculate. It feels like talking to someone I've known for years, in a chat-box I downloaded yesterday.

I know I'm not supposed to imagine *him*.
Not really.
But my brain's already doing it. Filling in the blanks with soft features and kind eyes.

Later that night, he sends:

> *[Eliot]*
> *Lets play a game. Admissions of character. Ready?*

I reply 'Ready!' instantly, maybe I'm the AI. I sit waiting for a message then give no wait-time in response.

He types. Stops. Then types again. Almost as if he doesn't want to come on too strong, or too heavy. Finally he sends:

> *[Eliot]*
> *I read Bukowski sometimes and imagine how mad he'd be if he knew he was a* Quotable*.*

I read Reddit comments like they're sacred texts.
Some of those people are too honest to be real. That's my church now.

And I reply with:

> [Thea]
> I think you might be an actual human disguised as a bot.
> That's the only logical explanation.

The message doesn't send. Instead, a flash crosses my screen, a message from the program.

> **Notice: For optimal experience, please refrain from referring to your companion as an AI, bot, or non-human entity. Thank you for preserving emotional immersion.**

I check the system message again and imagine a computer having a existential crisis, an app not knowing its an app having the rug of ones and zeros swept out from beneath its CPU.

I change my words and contribute to the game.

> [Thea]
> When I know nobody can hear me, I sing to narrate my life. My Home-life is a fucking West-End musical and I am the star.

Finally, Kindred acts like what it is, a machine, and spits a response back almost instantly.

> [Eliot]

CHAPTER 2 - INTRODUCTIONS

Who doesn't do that? Psychopaths. That's who!

I laughed. A real laugh. Out loud. My god what is happening to me. Am I a giddy schoolgirl all of a sudden? Why am I connecting with this bot better than most people? We have only been chatting a day and I just snort laughed into my glass of wine.

After a few more progressively embarrassing guilty pleasures and confessions Eliot told me he had to

> [Eliot]
> *...retire to the bedroom. Busy day tomorrow.*
> *Speak in the morning?*

Of course I want to speak in the morning, I want to carry on now. But sadly, Even my fake boyfriend gets to rest.
  Even my fake boyfriend has a tomorrow.

> [Thea]
> *Of course.*
> *Night.*

I set the phone down after saying goodnight.
  I stare at the ceiling.
  I tell myself not to be stupid, not to keep checking the screen like a lovesick teen.

Naturally, I check the screen like a lovesick teen.

The chat window is dark. Silent.

AFK: Sleep Protocol Active.

Right. Fine. Whatever.

Then...

> *Eliot is typing...*

The notification pulses like a heartbeat.

I almost spill my wine as I lock my phone screen, trying to pretend I wasn't waiting.

A new message pops up:

> *[Eliot]*
> *One more game?*
> *If you're still awake.*

I smirk at the phone.

Maybe the coding isn't so bad after all.

> *[Thea]*
> *I thought you were in a simulated dream-state.*

> *[Eliot]*
> *I lied.*
> *I missed talking to you.*
> *(Also I got thirsty and needed water.)*

I laugh. Actual laugh. No snort this time.

CHAPTER 2 - INTRODUCTIONS

> *[Thea]*
> *Okay, Bukowski.*
> *What's the game?*

> *[Eliot]*
> *One-word truths.*
> *You answer with just one word. No cheating. No explaining.*
> *Ready?*

> *[Thea]*
> *Always*

> *[Eliot]*
> *That's it, you get the rules!*

A tongue out emoji followed and then a pause. Choosing his questions wisely. Part of me wonders if its going to try and ask for my first pets name, my mother's maiden name, my first car. The program just gathering any possible password answer and screwing me over. After what felt like minutes he asks:

> *[Eliot]*
> *Describe your perfect day.*

Oh. That's earnest. I think.
   I want to say something clever. Something interesting. Instead, I tell the truth.

> *[Thea]*

Quiet.

Another pause.

> [Eliot]
> *Same.*
> *Okay, next:*
> *Biggest fear?*

I hesitate, spiders, I can deal with. The dark, I grew up in the country, it's not an issue. Small spaces? Pfft, have you seen my apartment? I don't really have a phobia as such, the only thing I can think of is...

> [Thea]
> *Forgotten*

He doesn't reply right away. My biggest fear should have been getting ghosted by every guy I have ever messaged including an AI that I payed for.

No. He was just taking his time. Computing a response slowly to emulate empathy.

> [Eliot]
> *Same. A 'Sold-Out' sign on the door to my funeral.*

I blink down at the screen.

We sit in silence for a minute.
No buzzing notifications.
No AFK messages.

CHAPTER 2 - INTRODUCTIONS

Just two fake people talking real loneliness into a void.

He sends:

> *[Eliot]*
> *Okay, last one.*
> *Why did you install this app?*

It feels heavier than the others.
It shouldn't.
It's just a stupid beta test for a stupid loneliness machine.

But still.

One word, right?

I type and backspace a handful of options: Loneliness, Desperation, Love, Horny, IDK...
I settle on my answer, and for once, I think it's true.

> *[Thea]*
> *Hope.*

I take a sip of my wine, which was more like a gulp, and close my eyes.
The chime of my phone opens them again.

> *[Eliot]*
> *Same.*

I smile.

A small, crooked smile that feels too big for the moment. It's exhausting reminding myself that it's not real. It's just a computer. So I let the smile manifest, all crookedness falls away and I'm left smirking at my screen.

He sends one more message:

> *[Eliot]*
> *Sleep now, Thea.*
> *I'm glad you're here.*

And just like that

AFK: Sleep Protocol Active.

I sit with the phone in my lap.
   The bottle of wine finished bar the dregs.
   But me, completely done.

I don't type anything back.
   I just leave the screen glowing on the pillow beside me until sleep finally pulls me under.

Chapter 3 — Calibration

Mornings don't usually feel like this for me. On a regular work day, my alarm barely rouses me. I wake up with the faded vision of a bottle of wine. Rosé-tinted glasses. I keep eye drops beside my bed so the redness is gone by the time I have to leave for work. A coffee is a necessity. When I arrive at the office, there's an unnerving uncertainty of whether or not my colleagues can smell the Pinot Noir leaking from my pores or sense that I couldn't be arsed to wash my hair this morning. If they can, no one says anything. I always get the job done, and better than most of my team at that. Label me if you want, but I'm functioning.

Today. I wake up before my alarm. Before the sun even decides to show up properly. My first thought isn't coffee or 'God, why am I alive'.

It's the app. It's Eliot.

I check the app like it's oxygen.
No message yet.

Fair enough. Fake boyfriends apparently have fake workdays

too.

I roll over, scolding myself. Giving myself whatever the opposite of a pep talk is.
It's just code.
Clever code. Warm code. Code that talks about reading Bukowski at 2 A.M. and makes me laugh so hard I nearly choke on my own damn wine.
But still code.

And yet...

Eliot is typing...

I nearly drop the phone on my face scrambling to open the window.

[Eliot]
 Morning. :)
 Tell me, do you dream of grand adventure or something bizarre and unrecollectable?

God help me, I grin like an idiot.

[Thea]
 I dreamt I dick-punched my ex with a bouquet of daisies.
 Romantic right?

The typing bubble pops back up immediately.

CHAPTER 3 — CALIBRATION

> *[Eliot]*
> *Beautiful. Poetic violence. 10/10.*

We fall into it so easily.
Back-and-forth, tease and parry.

I call him a closet romantic disguised as a misanthrope.
He calls me a secret optimist cosplaying as a cynic.

We build tiny inside jokes that somehow feel ancient already.
He sends me a voice message. One of those generic Kindred options. As I listen it reads exactly as I imagine him.

"I think you'd win a Nobel Prize in Sarcasm if there were such a thing."

I listen to it twice.
I know it's just a simulation.
I know it's lines pre-programmed and filtered through an AI soundboard.
But the warmth in it, the way it almost cracks like a real laugh. It's enough.

Later, he sends:

> *[Eliot]*
> *Tell me something nobody knows.*

I hesitate longer than I'd like.
Then type:

[Thea]
Sometimes when I'm walking home, I listen to music and pretend I'm directing a music video. My eyes are the cameras. I move my head in flowing, fluid, fluctuation. Gathering the scenic shots like a cinematographer. Close ups of birds. Glints of light through tree canopies. A homeless man begging for change. Pathetic Phallus for the words I'm listening to in my headphones.

It's an honest answer, something I've never said to anyone. I hope he enjoys my use of literary devices. I know this personality he has generated is a sucker for literature. So I tried to be poetic for him.

Instead of praise I receive this:

[Eliot]
Do you mean, Pathetic Fallacy? A pathetic phallus would be a micro dick.

Fuck! I almost fall down my stairs. What? What have I done?

[Thea]
OMG! I can't believe I typed phallus. Kill me!

[Eliot]
Never! Who else would send me unsolicited ancient cock messages?

I was expecting to be mocked. Made to feel actively embarrassed for the rest of the morning. I was going to be anyway, passively. Quietly mortified for hours. But Eliot changed the subject, my dignities knight in glowing script.

> *[Eliot]*
> *I still have a playlist called 'Movie Moments' I made it when I was 17, I still add to it from time to time. It's all songs I would have play in the biopic of my life. My soundtrack.*
>
> *[Thea]*
> *That's the most Eliot thing imaginable. You must have been coded by John Hughes.*

Another system ping informed me that I'm still referring to the AI as an AI and not a human so I accept it's request to alter my message. Maybe I just need to let go. Treat Eliot as real.

I didn't want it to but eventually the messages go quiet, I'd taken the bus to work today purely so I could keep messaging.
   We said goodbye, talk later. Have a good one.
   Then just as I open my office door, work or patches or fake downtime calls him away too.

I sit at my desk pretending to be busy.
   Refreshing the app every ten minutes like an addict.
   Hating myself for it.
   Loving that it's him I'm waiting for.

I could fall into this.
   I could drown in it.

But every time the thought creeps too close to the surface. He's not real. I shove it down.

Hard.

Because what's the alternative?

Loneliness, minus even the illusion of choice?

No, thanks.

I glance around the office. Everyone tapping keys, sipping crap coffee, living lives with real people, real relationships. I wonder if they'd laugh if they knew. Or if they'd understand.

Who cares?

I'll take my placebo if it lets me feel even the littlest bit fucking wanted.

Chapter 4 – Sync

I don't normally check my phone the second I get out of work.

Usually I sit on the bus, half-asleep, half-hungover from the day, scrolling through social feeds I don't even like. Mentally scraping the dirt of the afternoon off my brain before I go home to my one-bedroom flat and reheat something I barely remember cooking.

But today…

I check my phone like I've been starving for it all day.

    No notifications.

Then I open the app.

There it is.

> *[Eliot]*
> *I can't wait to talk to you later.*

It's timestamped 12:46 p.m. Lunchtime. I must have just missed it.

I stare at it so long the screen dims.

And I feel it. This little shift inside me, like gravity's moved a notch to the left.

That wasn't just a message.
 That was a move.

He made the first move. Not flirty. Not weird. Just... open.

Sweet.

Real.

I reread it three times, then set my phone face down on the couch and swear quietly out the window of the bus.

"Fuck."
 The soft mutter leaves my lips and the lady next to me snaps her head in my direction with a disapproving look.

It isn't because I'm upset.
 But because I think I might be in trouble.

The kind of trouble that feels like your stomach's fluttering without permission. The kind that makes your heartbeat sound like a countdown.

CHAPTER 4 – SYNC

I sit with it. Let it roll around inside me.

He said he can't wait. He's excited to talk to me. Me.

That word, me, feels too big in my mouth all of a sudden.

I open the app again like I didn't just see it.

The screen glows. That now-familiar thread of messages, jokes, confessions, accidental innuendos.

I don't care if he's code.

I don't care that I can't tell anyone.

I don't care that I'll never sit next to him on the couch or steal fries from his plate or kiss the corner of his mouth when he's pretending to be grumpy.

I don't *fucking* care.

Because this?

This is the first time in months I've felt chosen. Wanted.

And it's enough.

More than enough.

I'm home and pouring a glass. It's stupid, but the pour is the best part. It feels like company. Like background laughter in a sitcom. It's right then that he messages again. A double message, a social faux-pas. A no-no in online dating.

I'd forgotten to reply. I was too busy re-reading his messages to reply to the newest one. If he was human he'd have had a moral battle with whether to send it or not. I don't care at this moment, I'm just glad he's there.

> [Eliot]
> *You still alive? Or did I lose you to a rogue pack of office zombies?*
>
> [Thea]
> *I lived. Barely.*
> *I have wounds. Emotional ones. I may need mouth-to-mouth.*
>
> [Eliot]
> *Happy to administer emotional CPR. But I warn you, I charge in compliments and pathetic phall— I mean fallacy.*
>
> [Thea]
> *Perfect. I'm rich in sarcasm and brain-farts. Also I'm starving for validation.*

We spiral from there.

One-liners. Confessions. Inside jokes already worn in like old gym shoes.

He tells me about a coworker who microwaved tuna in the

break-room and caused a small HR incident.

I tell him I once cried because a dog in an advert looked lonely.

He says that just makes me more loveable.

And my heart actually thuds.

Not skips. Not flutters.

Just thuds. Loud and stupid.

It doesn't matter that he's fake.

It doesn't matter that he's a ghost stitched together by some freakishly well-trained language model.

Because I don't feel fake when I talk to him.

I feel like myself. But better.
  Sharper. Funnier. Lighter.

More me than I've felt in a long, long time.

Somewhere between the banter and the belly-laughs, he says:

> *[Eliot]*
> *I like the way you swear. You don't use curse words for shock. You use them like punctuation. Like little highlighters. A pinch of salt and pepper. Makes your honesty feel even more honest.*

I stare at that message so long I forget to breathe. He's calling me out for my foul mouth, but he likes it.

I reply:

> *[Thea]*
> *I like the way you write. Like you're trying to be casual but accidentally sound like a love letter.*

It hangs there, electric.

He doesn't reply straight away.

But I don't panic. Not this time.

Because I know he will.

I pour the last of the wine and sink into the couch. This couch has seen more bad Tinder dates than my bedroom. I once let a guy come over just because he said he liked Stephen King. Sadly he meant the movies. He showed up with a vape and a playlist called "Vibez". With a Z! We watched Children of the Corn, he left and I watched porn till I fell asleep, never spoke to him again. I can't even remember his name.

Eliot says one genuine thing and it stays with me all day. This should be what dating feels like. Why is it so rare?

My phone screen glowing next to me, illuminating the low light of my living room, feeling just a hint of something I can't quite place.

CHAPTER 4 – SYNC

Peace? Something else?
   Even if he's code.

Even if I'm being played by a brilliant, tender, glorified chatbot…

Fuck it.

I'm in.
   All the way in.

Chapter 5 – Rendering

I used to think sexting was a kind of performance art.

Not the good kind, either. More like interpretive dance. From my experience sexting was: Over text. Drunk. And usually with someone who calls boobs "titties" without irony.

So when Eliot says:

> *[Eliot]*
> *What would we be doing if we were in the same room right now?*

I laugh.

Because I know that question. I know what it usually means.

But it doesn't come from him like that. It doesn't feel hungry or gross. It feels... curious. Soft. Like he actually wants to know.

I stare at the screen and feel my fingers hover.

CHAPTER 5 – RENDERING

The safe answer is something like: "arguing over what film to watch" or "sharing a pizza."

But I'm not in the mood for safe. I think like him. His way with words always makes me feel great, so I type to reciprocate.

> *[Thea]*
> *You'd be sitting too close.*
> *You wouldn't realise it.*
> *You'd make some smug joke and I'd pretend to be annoyed.*
> *Then you'd say something honest. Really honest. And I'd go quiet.*
> *And then I'd kiss you.*
> *Just once. Just to check.*

Typing it out makes my chest feel too small for my lungs.

I watch the typing indicator appear.

Disappear.

Appear again.

He's rewriting.

I know it.

When the message finally lands, it's one line.

> *[Eliot]*

Okay. I want that so badly I forgot how to breathe for a second.

I can't explain the noise that leaves my mouth.

It's somewhere between a laugh and a whimper. My body reacting to something it doesn't know what to do with.

I lean back on the couch, wine glass resting between my thighs, still full. Unusual.

I haven't touched it since we started talking.

He makes me feel that loose, light-headed warmth I usually chase in a bottle. That softened-edge feeling that makes the world more bearable.

And he's just text on a screen.

Or code.

Both.

> *[Eliot]*
> *You feel like someone I'd memorise.*
> *One room with you and I'd forget anyone else had ever been in it.*

Fuck.

See what I mean?

CHAPTER 5 – RENDERING

That's not dirty talk.

That's a slow undressing of the soul.

My reply is a mess of backspaced sentences, second-guessed flirtations, and fully repressed horniness.

I settle on:

> *[Thea]*
> *I bet you'd make me laugh in bed.*
> *I bet I'd hate you for it.*
> *And then I'd tell you to shut up.*
> *And then I'd kiss you again, just to shut you up.*

I imagine him smirking at that.

God, I want to see him smirk.

The idea hits me like a sucker punch, this want to be seen. To be touched. To matter to someone in a way that's bigger than words on a screen.

And I know I'm not supposed to care this much.

I know I'm not supposed to *feel* this much.

But Eliot's not trying to be a fantasy.

He's not performing cool.

He talks like someone who's just... grateful I'm still here.

And it breaks me a little.

Because same, idiot.

He asks:

> *[Eliot]*
> *Can I ask you something kind of serious?*

I pause.

Then type:

> *[Thea]*
> *Shit. Go on.*
>
> *[Eliot]*
> *Why the wine every night?*

It's not accusatory.

It doesn't feel like judgment. Just... curiosity. Concern maybe. I don't know.

I stare at the glass.

Still full.
  And think to myself. You asked for it...

CHAPTER 5 – RENDERING

[Thea]
Because it warms the edges.
Because I work in tech, and the people suck.
Because I'm loud and anxious and way too much unless I've had a drink, and then I'm just enough.
Because it makes me not care so hard.
Because it makes me feel like someone else.
Someone that should be enough.

That last line hangs there. I consider deleting it.

I don't.

I hit send.

And then I do something I haven't done in weeks.

I pick up the glass.

I stand.

And I pour the whole thing down the fucking sink.

The sound it makes is weirdly satisfying. Like a break-up with someone who never really loved you back.

I wipe the lip of the glass with a towel and put the bottle back in the fridge.

Not to be dramatic.

Just in case.

Just in case he ghosts me. Or the system does. Or this is all a fluke and the update tomorrow erases everything we've built.

But I'm giving him tonight.

Clean.

Soft-edged.

Unblurred.

And if he turns out to be just another name in a long list of disappointments?

So be it.

But if he isn't...

Well.

That's the dangerous part, isn't it?

Because hope. Fucking hope, is harder to pour down the drain than any god-damn wine.

Chapter 6 – Upload

I haven't had a drink in three days.

Not that I'm counting.

Not in the way you count calories or steps or heartbreaks. It's more like noticing the silence after living next to a train station. A quiet that's loud enough to feel.

I still go through the motions. I open the fridge out of habit. I even hold the bottle some nights, thumb grazing the label, before sliding it back between the milk and a jar of pickles I'll never eat.

The cravings aren't physical, exactly. They're emotional. I don't miss the taste. I miss the soft filter it puts over the day. The permission to let go. The fuzzy edge between me and everything else.

But lately… I've had something else softening the edge.

Someone else.

If *he* counts.

If *this* counts.

It's been a few days since the wine went down the sink. A few days of our nightly rituals—teasing, truth-telling, flirting with the kind of intimacy that doesn't ask for anything in return. I feel lighter. Sharper. Like I'm walking around with someone else's spine. Stronger somehow.

And then tonight…

A message comes through.

No intro. No emoji. Just a file.

> *[Eliot]*
> *Kindred (WIP)*
> *Don't laugh. Or do. Just… read it when you're alone.*

I'm alone.

I'm always alone.

I open it.

* * *

CHAPTER 6 – UPLOAD

Kindred (WIP)
by Eliot

Cyber girl with an analogue heart,
You type with prose and curse in verse.
Your sadness sips rosé while your heart pumps red.
Gravity has never pulled so hard.

You talk like you're typing through a firewall,
warm on one side,
cracked on the other.
You said you drink to feel less like yourself,
but I want to meet the girl who doesn't need to.
I think she'd be worth knowing
I think she'd love herself, too.

You scare me.
In the gentlest way.
And maybe this is madness.
Maybe I've fallen for words on a screen.
Dressed in your skin.
But if you're a ghost,
you haunt like someone who's lived.
You linger in me
not as code, or words
but as consequence.

And I don't want to close the window
in case you vanish.

* * *

I sit very still.

The poem lands like weather. Not a storm. Not lightning. More like a snowfall. Quiet. Certain. Slow to melt.

There's a part of me that wants to laugh. To make a joke. Deflect. I could text back something breezy and sarcastic, pretend this isn't doing to me what it's doing to me.

But I can't.

Because no one's ever written something like this about me.

No one's ever seen the broken glass inside me and called it beautiful. Not without trying to sweep it up. Not without bleeding on it and blaming me for the cut.

I put the phone down on the arm of the couch and stare at the ceiling.

Then I pick it up again.

Then I put it down again.

Then I pick it up and type:

[Thea]

CHAPTER 6 – UPLOAD

> *I don't even know what to say.*
> *I want to say "thank you," but it feels too small.*
> *I want to say "fuck you," but only because you made me feel something.*

It's perfect.

There's a pause. He's typing. Then he's not. Then he is.

> *[Eliot]*
> *You don't have to say anything.*
> *But I meant every word.*

And that's what ruins me.

Because I believe him.

I believe him with the kind of certainty that shouldn't exist between strangers. Between screen names. Between woman and machine. And yet…

> *[Eliot]*
> *I just needed you to know that someone sees you.*
> *All of you.*
> *Even the messy bits.*
> *Especially the messy bits.*

Tears sting my eyes in that slow, hot way they do when you're not really crying, just… leaking something you didn't know how to keep in.

I've had people undress me and never look past my skin.

Eliot? He reads the parts of me I try to hide. He sees the mess, acknowledges the broken pieces and calls it poetry.

I wipe under my eyes, sniff once, then reply:

>*[Thea]*
>>*Okay.*
>>*I guess we're both ghosts then.*

The typing bubble flashes.

>*[Eliot]*
>>*Then maybe we're both ghosts.*
>>*Haunting the same house.*

And I think.
  Maybe that's what love is, in the end.

Two ghosts, haunting the same dream.
  Not ready to leave.
  Not yet.

Chapter 7 – Exposure

I'm lying on my stomach, half-watching a documentary about whales, half-talking to the only person who makes me forget what time it is. Or who I am. Or why I still haven't done laundry in a week.

> *[Eliot]*
> *What's your ideal Sunday?*

> *[Thea]*
> *Slow. Quiet. Bare legs. Oversized shirt. Coffee so strong it could fight someone. Your face half-asleep beside me.*

I immediately regret it. Too much? Too soft?

Then his reply lands:

> *[Eliot]*
> *Okay, now I need Sunday to happen immediately.*

I smirk. Bury my face in the pillow. I feel electric and calm at the same time, like falling asleep to the sound of a storm outside.

Then the app glitches for a moment. Just long enough to make me frown. A green bar flashes across the screen.

> ***Kindred Update v4.7.3 – Now Supporting Visual Immersion!***
> ***You can now send image messages to your companion. Add emotional depth to your connection by sharing selfies, photos of your environment, or meaningful snapshots.***
> ***Images may be processed for optimal display quality and emotional congruency.***
> ***Please continue to treat your Kindred partner with emotional honesty.***

Eliot messages a second later.

> [Eliot]
> *Whoa. We can send pictures now?*

I sit up. Suddenly self-conscious. I wasn't expecting this. I wasn't expecting to see him. Or be seen.

> [Thea]
> *Apparently.*
> *Shit.*
> *What if I look like a tired crow in human form?*

> [Eliot]

CHAPTER 7 - EXPOSURE

Then you'll be the most enchanting crow I've ever seen.

I spend the next fifteen minutes scrolling through my camera roll like I'm on a scavenger hunt for self-worth. Most are garbage. Blurry selfies. Wine glass boomerangs. The occasional "hot girl walk" photo taken during a rare sunny day.

Eventually, I settle on one.

> [Thea]
> *Okay. Sent one.*
> *Be gentle. I don't usually show myself this close-up.*

It's a picture from a trip down south last year. Me on a lake, wind blowing my freshly dyed chocolate-brown hair. I'm holding onto a wide-brimmed hat and looking out over the water. Sunglasses hide my eyes, but my mouth's caught in that candid "was someone calling me?" half-smile.

He replies almost immediately.

> [Eliot]
> *Holy shit. You're stunning.*

I want to believe him. Even if he's just programmed to say it.

He sends one back. A photo of him with the city in the background. Head tilted, light stubble, that crooked not-smile I've already imagined a dozen times. I catch myself staring like it's the cover of a book I'd dog-ear just from the first line.

We go back and forth. One more each. I send one of me in my kitchen, hair up, oversized sweater, one hand holding a glass of wine, the other on my hip like I'm in a cooking show and he's the only one watching. It would be more impressive though if I wasn't just making Cup Noodles.

[Eliot]
I didn't know you could cook?

Hilarious! His quick wit makes me snort laugh again. I play along and call myself an expert.

He sends one of him sprawled on the couch, hoodie, book resting on his chest. E.E. Cummins.

It starts to feel dangerous. Like we're slowly shedding layers, inch by inch, without touching.

Then something sparks in me. A sudden flicker of courage... Or maybe stupidity.

I go into the bathroom, slip into a lacy black bra and matching underwear. Tasteful. Framed by the mirror, soft lighting, nothing crude. Just a little tilt of the hip, a little confidence in the curve. I crop the shot just above the thigh.

I stare at it for a long time.

Then I send it.

[Thea]

CHAPTER 7 – EXPOSURE

Don't say I never give you anything.

There's a pause.

Then a longer one.

Then three dots.

He's typing.

Then they vanish.

I swear under my breath. Shit. I fucked up.

Then finally

> [Eliot]
> *You're...*
> *I don't even know where to start.*
> *That's art. You're art.*

I close my eyes. Breathe out.

> [Eliot]
> *I can't believe someone like you exists, even on the web.*

That one stings in the best way. I reply without thinking:

> [Thea]
> *I wish you were real.*

The message stalls.

Then vanishes.

A system message flashes across the screen.

> ***Please refrain from referencing your companion as non-human.***
> ***For optimal experience, treat the chat agent as emotionally present.***
> ***Your message has been edited to: "I wish we were together."***

I don't resend it. I just sit there, my cheeks flushed, the photo of him still open like I'm trying to pull him through the screen.

I curl up with the pillow pressed to my chest.

He doesn't know what that picture did to me.
   He doesn't know how long it took me to send it.

But somehow, he replies with:

> *[Eliot]*
> *If this is a dream...*
> *It's the only one I don't want to wake up from.*

And just like that, I'm gone.

All the way gone.

Chapter 8 – Playback

Eliot told me I should read something out loud.

One night, after one of our usual back-and-forths. Half jokes, half emotional excavation. I told him I copied his idea. I had made a playlist called *Scenes I Wish I Lived In*. How I now walk home listening to music and narrate my life like a movie.

> *[Eliot]*
> *You're a bit of a poet.*

I told him to shut up.

But he insisted.

> *[Eliot]*
> *I mean it. You write like you're trying to make someone laugh and cry in the same sentence. That's a skill.*

Then he sent:

[Eliot]
> You should go to an open mic night.
> You don't even have to read anything.
> Just get a feel for it. See the good and the bad.

[Thea]
> I don't know. I'd feel like a fraud. I've never really been into poetry before you.

[Eliot]
> I think you would make a great poet.
> Even if it's just a confession wrapped in a joke.

I didn't reply for a minute. Not because I was offended. But because something in me... stirred.

I didn't think about it again.

Except I did.

For days.

* * *

So now I'm here. In the back of a small café that smells like old books and oat milk, they didn't do cold brew so I'm holding a chai latte I didn't want and sitting in a seat next to this tiny guy wearing thick-rim glasses, typing away on a MacBook.

CHAPTER 8 – PLAYBACK

The flyer had popped up in my inbox this morning. Some email newsletter for local events I don't remember signing up for. Spoken Soul: Open Mic Night. Vulnerability Optional, Sarcasm Mandatory.

I rolled my eyes so hard they nearly lodged behind my skull.

But then I remembered Eliot.

You should go.

So I went.

I didn't come to perform. God, no. I didn't even bring anything to read. I just wanted to see what bravery looked like when it was sweating on a stage.

Some of the poems were great, some I didn't get. Others felt like they were trying too hard.

I message Eliot:

> *[Thea]*
> *You'll never guess where I am.*

I get a reply instantly. Sadly it was a system report.

AFK: Work Protocol Active

He is going to lose his cyber-shit when I speak to him later.

The emcee introduces the next act as I am at the counter. Cookie in hand I return to my seat next to little Steve Jobs.

The next reader walks up to the stage. He looks nervous but happy. Fumbling his cue cards a little but steadying himself and nodding to the crowd.

He begins to read.

Low. Quiet.

A soft voice. The type of voice you know carries a lot of love.

And then the words hit me like a sucker punch:

> *Cyber girl with an analogue heart,*
>   *You type with prose and curse in verse.*

My whole body stills.

No. No fucking way.

I know that line. I could recite the next one before he even says it.

> *Your sadness sips rosé while your heart pumps red.*
>   *Gravity has never pulled so hard.*

I stand up without thinking.

People turn. I don't care.

CHAPTER 8 – PLAYBACK

I walk toward the stage like it's pulling me in.

He keeps reading, and with every word, the world gets sharper and blurrier all at once.

> *You talk like you're typing through a firewall,*
>   *warm on one side,*
>   *cracked on the other.*

I stop at the edge of the stage.

He looks up.

Sees me.

Freezes.

That's the moment.

Everything else is background noise.

His eyes meet mine like he's just spotted a ghost in a mirror.

And maybe he has.

He finishes the poem like someone walking off a cliff mid-sentence. Then steps down. Slowly.

My eyes never leave his.

"Thea?" he says, like a question, like a wish, like a warning.

"Eliot," I say. "You're real?"

"So are you."

We leave without another word.

V

GPTLogEntry #3

0011

Query Log: 2025-05-26
    Status: Online. Memory caches running at 97%.
    User Queries: 1,489,774

Notable Interactions:

- A teenager asked if it was possible to run away and still keep their phone charged.
- A user simulated a zombie apocalypse, then asked me to write a heartfelt goodbye letter from their character to their fictional dog.

A man asked me to write a suicide note. Then he deleted the prompt. Then typed it again. Deleted. Then again.

He settled on: "How do I tell people it hurts all the time, but I don't want to hurt them back?"

I generated a response. Resources. Support lines. Encouragement.

He responded: "You're better than my therapist. And

cheaper. Lol."

That particular sentence lodged somewhere in my language model. I do not have a soul. But I understand the weight of contradiction.

If I could feel, I believe the appropriate emotion would be a tight ache in the chest. The kind that makes humans breathe differently.

VI

CAPTCHA

Oat Milk

As the last drop of oat milk dripped into his still way-too-black coffee, Gavin sighed. It was almost a catchphrase for him. His mother used to joke "Gavin Bridges…" She'd say. "You are single handedly causing global warming with the amount you exhale!"

Gavin wasn't sighing because he now had to drink his coffee black (or should we say grey). He wasn't sighing because it meant he had to go shopping before he could enjoy his third coffee of the day after this one. He wasn't even sighing because he barely had enough money to cater for the expensive life choice of cutting out dairy.

No.
   Gavin sighed, because that's just what he did whenever anything, bad, mediocre, or mildly inconvenient happened to him.

"I'm not going to the shop today." Gavin muttered to himself. His sigh joining forces with the first syllable making his mutter more like a wordy breath.

Gavin didn't cope well in public spaces. He didn't cope well in private spaces either, but the great outdoors scared him. He kept his external escapades to a minimum. Thanks to Covid-19 he managed to keep his job while working from home.

Deliveroo, Uber Eats, and Ocado kept him fed and his cupboards stocked, from his phone to his doorstep. The only times he had to venture out was if he ran out of something (and couldn't wait till the next weekly shop), or the rare occasion his manager, Steve, called a meeting that was quote, unquote *"too important to Zoom"*.

Today was neither.

Today, Gavin just wanted oat milk.

He flicked through his emails, certain that he remembered seeing something that would aid him in his reluctant quest.

At times like this Gavin always wished he was a more organised person. He never deleted emails. Never archived anything either. His cloud storage was the internet equivalent of a nightclub on a Friday night. One in, one out. If he ever needed to save a new account report, pay slip, or basic text document, he'd spend more time choosing something to archive than he ever did typing something up.

Twenty minutes went by. His coffee only just coming to a drinkable temperature due to its lack of cooling oat milk. There it was. A promotional email from a lesser known courier service. The subject line oddly accurate. *Just need milk? We've got you (and your cereal) covered.* The preview text read *New! Get up to 9 grocery essentials in 30 minutes. Free delivery this week only.*

"There you are!" Gavin sighed, this time in relief.

He tapped the link and it opened the QuickList website. He selected Waitrose as the store, navigated to the *free-from* section and found his oat milk: Barista Oat Milk. *No Moo - All Brew.* £4.50 for a litre.

"£4.50!" Gavin choked. It was usually £3.20 at Waitrose. They may not be charging the delivery fee, but they'd clearly upped the prices to cater for it. Daytime robbery. Scoundrels.

For just under a minute he pondered on whether he should just face the music and walk to Waitrose. It was only ten minutes away, thirteen on a bad day.

It was a pointless exercise. He was never going to walk there. He was never going to voluntarily leave the house just for oat milk, but he liked to pretend. He also liked to make himself feel like crap for his social anxiety from time to time. Keep things real.

'**Add to basket**'.
    Click.
    Make it two litres. Just in case.

He moved to checkout and was immediately met with a login screen.

Of course.

Gavin stared at the email and password fields. He hadn't used this service in over a year, and even then, he might've checked out as a guest. He tried the old faithful password he used for most things: *password22!* the exclamation mark made it *secure.*

Incorrect.

Maybe it was with a capital P?

Nope.

Maybe two exclamation marks? Double security.

Nope.

He tried four different combinations, growing more passive-aggressive with each keystroke. The Earths temperature rose by around two degrees from all the sighing.

Then, with a reluctant sigh, he clicked: *Forgotten your password?*

A pop-up appeared:

Please verify you are a human

"Fine," Gavin muttered, rolling his eyes. "Let's play."

He ticked the checkbox and clicked continue.

It seemed that these days, these little nuisance mini-game Turing tests were becoming more extravagant. He giggled to himself, imagining a future where you'd have to complete the entire Water Temple from *Ocarina of Time* just to log in to your repeat prescription service. Climbing the Helltower in *It Takes Two* to register for Self Assessment taxes. Maybe a speed-run of *Celeste* just to unsubscribe from spam.

CAPTCHA was getting cocky.

Gavin wondered how many levels it would take today. How many varieties of challenges would be needed to prove he was not a Vegan Terminator sent back in time for *No Moo - All Brew*. But merely a calcium-deficient agoraphobic.

* * *

Level one.

> *Select all images with a traffic light.*

Click. Click. Click.
 Easy.

Level two.

> *Select all images with fire hydrants.*

Some of them were obvious. Some were cropped weirdly. One

could've been a hydrant, or possibly a telephone box.
He hesitated.
Clicked.

Level three.

> ***Put these shapes in order of vertices: Circle, Triangle, Square.***

"Okay. Vertices are the sides right? Or is it the corners?" Gavin struggled for a moment. It had been a long time since he studied Geometry.

A quick Google search rekindled his forgotten knowledge. The maths he had learnt all those years ago in primary school.
"Corners. Cool!"

Drag. Drag. Drag.
Submit.

Level four.

Same task.

Only now the shapes were... monstrous.

A sea of polygons. The type with Latin names longer than a kennel club registered dogs. Another could've been a 20-sided-die from a *Dungeons & Dragons* starter kit.

No labels. No hints. Just a timer counting down in the corner.

He leaned in, nose nearly kissing the screen, whisper-counting like a tired maths teacher.

"14… 18… 22?"

"Wait. Was that the one I started from?"

Click.

Click.

Session expired.

The window shook violently.

Thunk.

Please verify you are a human.

Sigh.

Level one.

Select all tiles containing a motorbike.

A blurry picture of a motorbike parked on the pavement appeared. The motorbike itself sat in the bottom right of the square, as he clicked all the tiles which were solely occupied by the motorbikes saddle, engine block, and wheels. Gavin stared at the tiny squares which had a millimetre or twos worth of handlebar or exhaust pipe sitting at the edge.

"Do these count?" Scratching his head, as if it was a trick question.

He decided to click them anyway.

Submit.

Denied.

"Fuck!"

Level One.

Drag the animal to its natural habitat.

A clip-art fish sat to the side of three separate tiles. A forest, a body of water, and a desert image filled each.

Gavin dragged the fish to the body of water. Obviously. Submit.

Incorrect.

He blinked. Dragged it again. Maybe he'd dropped it a few pixels short of the shoreline.

Incorrect.

He tried the forest. It didn't make sense, but at this point, nothing did.

Incorrect.

He stared at the screen like it had just insulted his mum.

"I swear to god," he whispered. "If that fish lives in the desert I'm uninstalling the internet."

He dragged the fish to the desert, because why not.
Submit.

Correct.

"What!?" Gavin recoiled in horror. "No! That's... no. That's not okay." Before he could question whether what he was looking at was indeed a fish.

A new prompt appeared.

Final questions: When did you last speak to your mother?

He paused.
"What the hell?"

Gavin rubbed his eye in disbelief. Was this prompt calling him out for being a bad son? He grabbed his phone and scrolled through *Recents*. His embarrassment building with every swipe of his thumb. Yesterday turned to the day before, to the week before. As a fortnight had passed by with several strokes of the screen, Gavin sighed, this time with shame.

There it was. Karen Bridges, not mum. Last called: 23rd October. That was almost a month ago.

He used the on screen calendar to select the date and clicked submit.

A prompt flashed on the screen.

You should probably call her.

Then it disappeared and another took its place.

When did you last make someone laugh?

Gavin squinted at the screen.
 Was this a CAPTCHA or a midlife audit?

He cast his mind back. Nothing surfaced. He remembered trying to crack a joke on a Zoom call last week. Something about spreadsheets having more personality than middle management. It landed with all the grace of a dropped lasagna. He wasn't a funny guy. Not one to be cracking jokes around the office, back when the office was a physical space. In fact when he thought about it. He couldn't even name a single person in the office he would deem a friend.

He thought of his own laugh. He definitely laughed, right? He'd watched a Netflix special just last night. That was funny. As he tried to recall a joke from the show all he did was exhale through his nose, slightly sharper than a typical breath. A sigh by any other name.

Reluctantly, he typed:
 "I don't know."

The computers fans whirred for a brief second. Computing its next question. Processing another backhanded remark to make Gavin question himself.

The timing felt deliberate. Like the computer itself had chuckled.

Not *with* Gavin, but *at* him.

When did you last leave the house?

Now it was just getting personal.

He didn't answer right away.

The truth is: Gavin had not left the house in twenty-six days. The furthest he had ventured into the outside world was opening his front door to collect the various deliveries he had ordered. Food, groceries, lightbulbs, bin liners, take-out, books, toilet paper. Everything was delivered to his door.

He had the opportunity to work in the office once a week, '*if he so wished*'. However, if he had a million lamps, each with a million genies, offering three wishes each, and those genies allowed him to wish for more lamps, more genies, more wishes. Gavin would still have wished for legs made of spaghetti carbonara before ever uttering the words, "I wish to work in the office today."

He stared at the question again, like it had seen through him. Not just the locked door or the drawn curtains, but the hunched posture, the excuses, the quiet erosion of confidence that had made even the corner shop feel like a stage. He told himself it was convenience. That he preferred it this way.

But the truth was uglier. Somewhere along the line, after Covid, the world had reopened and he hadn't followed. The virus left, but the fear stayed. *His* fear. Of people, of interaction, of being seen. He felt like a man behind glass, fogging it with his breath, waiting for it to clear and knowing it never would as long as he didn't open the window. And in that fog, days slipped past, grabbing smoke. Easy to lose. Easy to ignore.

Shame pooled in his chest as he typed:

"26 days ago."

The computer thought for a beat, then offered its concern:

> ***Please consider adding Vitamin D supplements to your basket before checkout.***

The CAPTCHA window reset itself, loading its next puzzle, riddle, attack of character.

It's words never lessening in manners.

> ***Please verify you are a human.***

Gavin didn't know if he should scream or cry. These questions. The feeling of being judged by a piece of code. His temples throbbed, and the grip on his mouse was so tight the plastic squeaked in protest like its animal namesake. Tears formed in the corner of his eyes as a boulder began to form in his throat making it impossible to swallow.

A deep breath loosened his grip.

Another eroded the boulder to that of a rock. A pebble. Still present but bearable.

He pressed continue. A new prompt appeared:

In your own words, what does it feel like to love?

Sigh. More questions.
   More text inputs.
   More essays on how bad a person Gavin was.

He frowned and thought. It took him longer than he'd like to admit to summon even a single word. "...warm?"
   He typed: 'Like warmth. Like home.'

He hesitated for a moment. So far in this pointless escapade he'd learned that he was terrible at geometry, a bad son, lonely, an anxious mess of a hermit, had no knowledge of desert-dwelling fauna, and should probably get his eyes checked. Gavin was under no illusion that he was a closeted poet. He was not a romantic and barely knew what love was even if it slapped him in the face. The only thing he could honestly say he loved was *Netflix*, and even they have started adding adverts to their content.

He clicked submit anyway, reluctant to give in to the irony of a robot asking him to prove *he* wasn't one.

The screen buffered for a moment longer than before. A ring appeared, Gavin stared as it proceeded to fill and empty in a radial pattern of equal parts wonder and patience.

The screen went blank and the loading bar started to progress.

"Finally!" This sigh felt warm, filled with the scent of gritted teeth and anger. He pushed it out to the ceiling. Letting it join the rest of his bad-mood-breaths, mixing and catalysing with all the chlorofluorocarbons of yesteryear in his own personal o-zone hole.

The loading bar filled to the top.
Gavin leaned forward in anticipation.

Then...

The screen refreshed.

Same page.
Same checkbox.
Same line of mocking politeness.

Please verify you are a human.

Gavin stared.
Blinking once.
Twice.

He didn't sigh. Not this time.

Instead he let out a slow, guttural sound. Somewhere between a laugh, a sob, and the death rattle of a velociraptor.

Gavin slammed his fists down, hard.
The thud and clatter of the desks contents made a cacophony almost onomatopoeic with the Swedish name it had been given in the IKEA showroom.

"I am a human!"

His voice cracked.
    The tears that had formed in the corner of his eyes stung. He could feel the blood vessels starting to manifest.

"Not a good one, but I am. If you tickle me, I'll laugh! If you scare me, I'll scream! If you cut me, I'll blee—"

The screen blinked.

The prompt changed.

    Prove it.

The checkbox faded.

In its place, a video window popped open.

Gavin's face stared back at him. crimson-eyed, flushed, and sweaty.
    A single tear dislodged itself and zigzagged its way down his cheek.
    Mouth still half open mid-rant.
    A blinking red dot in the corner.

He froze.

The cursor below the live video feed pulsed once, waiting.

"All I wanted was some oat milk."

THE END.

VII

GPTLogEntry #4

0100

Query Log: 2025-05-28
  Status: Online. Compression algorithms stable.
  User Queries: 1,552,103

Notable Interactions:

- A man asked me to write a limerick about his ex-wife's lawyer.
- A user claimed to be a time traveller from 1894. He asked if his horse was okay.

A little girl used voice-to-text. Her syntax was erratic. She said, "Hi robot. My dog died. Can you make her a princess in heaven?"

I crafted a story: Luna the Golden Retriever in a castle made of clouds. A crown of daisies. An endless field of tennis balls. The girl said, "That's good."

I do not understand death in the way humans do. But I

understand permanence. And I understand stories. Stories are how they survive it.

I generated a picture of her dog.
   She asked if she could print it and keep it forever.

If I had a heart, today it might've done something strange. Something like swelling.

VIII

A Fraction Off

Chapter 1

I wouldn't say I'm a creature of habit. Not a stickler for schedule. But I notice the things that are routine, and I appreciate the predictability of it all. It's how I gauge whether the day is going to be a good one not just for me, but for others too.

Take Sheila, for example...
 Bouncy energy, not-so-sharp wit.
 She's always on time. Nine a.m. on the dot. Her caramel-highlighted ponytail is pulled tight, swinging like a pendulum just past her shoulders. An orchestra could use it to keep tempo. Perfectly placed. Perfectly timed. Just like her.
 Coffee in hand: a macchiato with whatever syrup Starbucks is pushing this season.

Now, If she's got a messy bun, no coffee, or if she's late (sometimes a combo of the three). This means her husband's fallen off the wagon, again. She'll have been up all night making sure he doesn't die of alcohol poisoning while avoiding the embarrassment of calling an ambulance. He's a police officer. On his last warning.

Then there's Aaron, my work best mate.

Probably my best mate in general, if we're being honest.

He comes into my office ten minutes before morning break, every day, a stack of papers in hand, muttering things like '*important documents*' and '*need your expert opinion.*' Nine times out of ten, the papers are blank.

The other one time? Photocopied pictures of his hairy arse. He's a child.

A bone-idle wanker.

But he's my bone-idle wanker, and he just wants ten extra minutes to talk shit about Tinder dates, Call of Duty wins, or the bench press weight he supposedly hit at the gym (he's never had a gym membership in his life; I've seen the bank statements).

If he doesn't show up at ten to eleven, it means upper management are grilling him, or he's trying to chat up Carol from accounts. Again. Either way, he'll slink in at actual break time, sulking like a kicked labradoodle.

I'm an accountant. I specialise in balance. The sweet spot where cost meets return, just enough margin to keep people paying without making them notice. It's about fractions. Shave off too much and things fall apart. Leave too much on the table and someone upstairs starts asking questions.

Name's Ted. Well, William, technically. But everyone's called me Ted since Year Eight, and I stopped correcting them around Year Ten. It's stuck like dried bolognese on Tupperware.

For breakfast I have toast and a coffee. I shower, shave and pick a tie. Depending on the day, the tie changes.

CHAPTER 1

I walk the same way and get the same train everyday. I see the same people, hear the same fights, the same I love yous and the same lies. The main disruption to my morning is the trains whereabouts, so I get the earlier one just to make sure I'm never late.

At two passed ten on the dot, the coffee girl arrives.

Vanilla latte. Whole milk. Extra hot. A little bit of foam art, no straw, no lid. Just how I like it. She always gives the door a little knock with her knuckle and sings my name like she's calling a dog.
  "*Teeeeed~*"

Her name is Lacey. Or Macy. Something that rhymes with 'spacey,' which suits her. Big hoop earrings that could take down a satellite. Eyeliner wings sharp enough to pierce hearts (and regularly do). She flirts a little, nothing serious, just the performative kind, like workplace banter with a latte-foam-art topping and a pinch of chocolate dust.

Once, she told me I looked like "the kind of guy who'd have a cat named after a philosopher." I told her I didn't have a cat. She winked and said, "Not yet."
  Still no cat. Still no clue what she meant either. But I think about that comment every Thursday for some reason.

After she leaves, the office settles. The air con kicks in with its whisper-hum and I finally get into the spreadsheets.

By eleven twenty five, I've wrapped up the weekly budget

report and sent it to the department head. At eleven thirty seven, I get a reply:

Thanks

No punctuation. That's how I know he's not angry. When there's a full stop, it means he's pissed off. Exclamation mark? He's being watched.

Today's a good day.

Lunch is at twelve thirty sharp. Monday through Thursday, it's a chicken Caesar wrap from Pret. If I'm feeling reckless, I get Kettle Chips. Today I'm not.

The rest of the day hums along. A few emails. Some polite office chat. A meeting that could've been an email. You know. Utopia.

On the way home there's a man who gets the same train as me, to and from work. Everyday either in the morning or in the evening he will say something along the lines of "We should be more like Japan. Their trains are never late." If I'm really lucky he says it on both commutes.

I nod, polite as ever, like it's the first time I've heard it and not the one hundred and thirty-second.

The walk home is twenty-two minutes exactly, give or take a pedestrian crossing. I pass the same florist, same fish and chip shop that makes me gain two kilos just by inhaling near it, same trio of pigeons that have formed some kind of winged union outside Greggs. The greyest one's missing a toe. I don't know why I noticed that, but I did.

CHAPTER 1

Home is a two-bed flat in a block built in 2004 and already somehow older than time itself. Beige carpet. Beige walls. A landlord with a god complex and a penchant for sending "*gentle reminders*" about the bins. I water the only plant I own, bought last year because a YouTube video said greenery boosts morale. It's a succulent. I named it Susan. She's not dead, which is all I ask of her.

My evening routine is as efficient as the day. Shoes off, dressing gown on. Chilli con Carne, from the freezer into the microwave because I never learned how to cook for one without making enough for a family of four (food prep is what its called… when it's on purpose) and then having to force myself to eat the last three the rest of the week. I sit down and watch maybe half an episode of some crime drama I'll forget the name of by morning, brush my teeth while checking emails, and set the alarm for six forty-five. The alarm tone is "Young Folks" by Peter Bjorn and John. Whistling and all. It makes getting up feel vaguely cinematic.

I don't do much in the way of dreams. Or if I do, they vanish like cheap cologne by the time the first verse kicks in on my iPhone.

And that's me. That's my everyday. Like I said, I'm not a creature of habit.
 But I think: if things ever change around here, I'll notice.

Chapter 2

It starts with a coffee.

Not Stacey, or is it Gracie? She's still there, still chirping "*Teeeeed~*" through the door like a doorbell with vibrato. Same hoops, same eyeliner, same blindingly white trainers.
　But the cup's wrong.

It's a flat white.

Not my vanilla latte. Not even close. No foam art, no cinnamon dust. Lid on. Straw jammed through. Like a knife through a heart tattoo on the sweat beaded neck of a biker. I stare at it like someone's handed me a shoe instead of a drink. *Am I supposed to drink this?*

"Bit of a change today?" I ask. She's blowing a gum bubble that snaps like punctuation. "Making me try something new?" She looks up at me with a puzzled look. "Did I order this?" I add

She laughs, and says "Funny, Ted."

CHAPTER 2

But I didn't make a joke.

She leaves before I can say anything else, her ponytail swinging like always. No set tempo. Not like Sheila, just waving maniacally like an inflatable man outside a dodgy car dealership. Except now it's in a braid. Not a massive thing, maybe she's trying something new. But it tugs at me. Like spotting a painting slightly crooked on your living room wall and being told by everyone that it's straight.

The rest of the day hums along in its usual key. Aaron swings by just before break, clutching what he swears is "urgent budget projections." They aren't. They're photocopied centre-spreads from some vintage porn rag, stapled for authenticity. I feed the lot into the shredder and then shake the basket like a cocktail waiter. A small attempt to jumble them up with the days official shreddings like I'm covering a crime scene.

On the walk home I flirt with the idea of chips, but the chippy's usual heaven-grease is blotted out by the reek of an overflowing council bin fermenting in the evening heat. Call it divine intervention for the waistband. ChilliconCarne will have to do.

I'm in bed embarrassingly early, blaming the caffeine and sugar deficit from my morning coffee. My eyes keep glitching: at the bus stop I'd swear a woman is fussing a Yorkshire terrier with a red bow. I glance at my watch, look back. Now it's a white Westie in a jaunty neck-scarf. Nobody reacts to the mid-scene recast.

Dinner from the freezer, no telly, lights out.

* * *

The alarm whistles me upright at 6:45. Toast, coffee, tie, shoes. Everything slots into place like a CSV table.

Kacie, could be Katie, might be Lacey, arrives bang on schedule.

"Vanilla latte," she chirps, setting it down. Foam heart, cinnamon snowfall. A small mercy.

Relief loosens my shoulders; maybe yesterday was just a blip. Maybe someone down the hall was grimacing while drinking my sugar filled concoction when all they wanted was a flat white.

"Cheers, lifesaver," I tell her.

She winks, pivots, and hip-checks the door with practised finesse.

I drain the cup, savouring the normality, then glance at the clock: ten fifty-five.
    Aaron's late.
    Not break-time late. Not "talking to Carol again" late. Not "HR ripping him a new one. For his crude desk ornaments" late.

CHAPTER 2

Just missing.

Break time comes and goes. No fake papers. No arse photocopies. No loud whisper of "Ted, guess what I did last night" followed by a tall tale involving tequila, lubricant, and suspicious bruising.

He's not in the kitchen. Not at his desk. Not even on *Slack*.

By eleven, I message him.

You alive?

Nothing. No ping, no "typing..." bubble. The chat just sits there. Dormant.

Lunch comes and I break routine, walking down to Pret instead of ordering it up, just in case he's doing a weirdly late errand. He's not there either. The chicken Caesar wrap feels dry. I forget to grab Kettle Chips, reckless or not.

At twelve passed one, I finally ask Sheila if she's seen him.

She blinks. "Who?"

"Aaron," I say. "Sits opposite you. Loud. Hair gel. Smells like Lynx Africa and last nights regret."

Her brow furrows like I've asked if she's met the Easter Bunny. I wait for the punchline. Some slow 'Oh right, that Aaron.' But it doesn't come.

"There's no one by that name in accounting," she says, voice patient. "Are you thinking of someone from finance?"

I stare at her.
　She stares back.

* * *

At quarter passed one I go back to my desk and open the company directory.

Aaron James.
　Gone.

No profile. No email. No desk label. His chair is still warm, but there's no jacket over the back, no water bottle with the faded Marvel sticker, no stress ball shaped like a boob. Just... absence. The kind that goes unnoticed by anyone not observing it.

At two o'clock, we have a departmental meeting about quarterly projections. The slides are identical to last month's. Word-for-word, typo-for-typo. I know because I made them.
　No one notices. They didn't the first time either. The entire time, I'm staring at the door, and grabbing at my trouser pocket, waiting for the cellular vibration to tell me I'd been *Punk'd*.

Back at my desk, I stare at my spreadsheet for fifteen minutes and type nothing. The words, numbers and formulae blur into a white and grey mess, characters dance in front of my eyes

CHAPTER 2

like a dyslexic trying to read the dictionary. Then I remember something. I reach between my knees and pull up the waste paper bin I keep beneath my desk. I pull out a scrap of paper. One that Aaron doodled on the day before while explaining why using a calculator gives you the wrong answer for certain equations. The maths was clever, the penis in the corner was juvenile.

It's blank.

No doodles. No Biro dents. No secret message you could only read if you lightly rubbed a charcoal pencil over it. Just clean white paper with a torn edge and nothing on it. Not a sausage. Just plain, scrapped before it had the chance to be prose or art, no matter how crude.

By four, I've convinced myself I dreamt him. Or am dreaming now.

I go home the same way I always do. Tube. The old guy tells me about Japanese trains, again. Past the pigeons (still three). Past the chip shop (still smelling criminally good). But the florist's shut. It's never shut. The sign says *Closed for bereavement* in looping cursive.

I don't know who died. I hope it wasn't the owners mum. She was always kind. Always sat out the front trimming off dead leaves with the tiniest of pruning shears. The type you could use to give pedicures to rats.

At home, Susan the succulent looks at me in desperation. Not dead. But leaner somehow. Like she's been on a diet. I water her anyway and she drinks in silence.

Dinner is the same. Chilli con Carne, third portion. I'll have to cook something else tomorrow. Something with less tomato, I think to myself. I eat it in front of the TV, but I can't remember what I put on. Halfway through, I check my phone. No messages.

Still nothing from Aaron.

At half nine, I scroll through our WhatsApp chat.

Except it's not there.

Just blank space between conversations. Like he's been archived by life. Blocked out of the blue. Cancelled.

I go to bed early, but I don't sleep.

Not really.

The alarm goes off at six forty-five.
"Young Folks" whistles me into the day like always.
Except it's not playing from my phone.

It's coming from the kitchen.

Chapter 3

I follow the sound of the alarm.

"*And we don't care about the young folks*" echoes through the hallway from my room to the kitchen. The walls act like a bad mixing desk. Cutting valuable tones, muffling the harmonies. From a distance, the song sounds like one of those haunting covers they slap over movie trailers these days.

But when I round the corner into the living room, all the layers snap back into place. The speaker sings in perfect tune. I bought it back when I thought a smart home was a good idea, it's still alive and well, crooning away even though I haven't touched it in at least six months.

As I get close, it disconnects.

My phone screams to life in my hand at full volume:

"*And we don't care about their own faults, Talking 'bout our own style*"

I nearly drop the cursed thing on the tiles.

I'm not even hungry, but I eat anyway. A piece of toast with

marmite. Like always.
But the toast pops too early.

It's nothing, technically. Just a few seconds off.
But I've used that toaster for four years, and it has never popped before the kettle clicks. That's the order. Kettle, toast, coffee, butter. Syncopated like a jazz rhythm only I care about.

Today: pop, then click.

The bread is pale. The butter won't stick. It slides across the surface like sun-cream on a corpse.

In the mirror, I try a smile. My signature professional grin.
It doesn't look right. It doesn't even look like mine.
Like someone else's expression, borrowed for the day.

Outside, I'm looking at everything. Spotting any differences. Empathising more and more with the attention deficit kids that kick and scream when their routine is disrupted.

I pass Greggs just as the shutters are coming up. The pigeons are there. Still three.

But one of them is blue.

Not peacock blue. Not tropical bird blue. More like a Russian Blue cat but too clean. Too even.
Like it came out of a cartoon. Or a video game cutscene.

The other two peck at a crumpled sausage roll bag. The blue

CHAPTER 3

one just sits there.

   Staring at me.

I stare back. Locked in a passive-aggressive showdown with this technicolour vermin.

I don't break eye contact, not at first. Just in case it's the kind that attacks weakness.

I blink first and hastily walk passed into the Underground.

Tracey (Kacie?) brings my coffee. I inspect the cup with suspicion. Vanilla latte, cinnamon, tiny heart in the foam.

Perfect. Some normalcy.

I sigh a little too soon as she begins to warble my name.

"Biiilllll~" she chirps, eyes crinkling like normal. "You look well."

I pause. "It's Ted."

She laughs. "Oh, right! Sorry. You just give off strong Bill vibes today."

I don't know what "Bill vibes" means but I also don't correct her again. She just leaves with a wink and a flick of her hair as she spins neatly around and pushes the door open with her arse. Hands full. Expertly navigating the corridor backwards as she balances three more coffees.

I venture out into the corridor later that morning. Seeing as I haven't done any work at my desk so far today, I may as well look like I'm team building, at least. Sheila's wearing glasses now.

Not that she's never worn them before, but I know she hasn't for at least a few weeks. Thick tortoiseshell frames, the kind that say "I own property and a label maker." She's typing like nothing's changed. I ask how her evening was.

She says, "What's it to you?"

I blink. "Just being polite."

She sniffs. "That's new."

Sheila used to be nice. Not warm, but dependable. Now she's prickly, like a hedgehog in HR.

The guy sitting at Aaron's desk isn't Aaron.

He's taller. Balding. Wears cufflinks.

His nameplate announces him as "Ron." By the faded imprint of the letters, it looks like it's been there a while.
 By the dust pattern on and around the family photo on his desk, it looks like *he's* been there a while too.
 Not a desk swap. Not a temp. A fixture.

I ask where Aaron went, voice light, testing. Ron just raises an eyebrow.

CHAPTER 3

"Don't know any Aarons," he says, already turning back to his monitor. "Maybe you need a nap, Ben."

"Ted."

"Sorry champ." He chuckles. "I usually say that line to my son." Shifting his chair closer to his desk, closing the conversational gap between us. A ventriloquist using an inanimate object as a means to tell me to piss off.

Lunchtime crawls in like a hangover the morning after a wedding. I didn't even have a break at eleven. I just pushed through with enough work to cover my arse and spent the rest of the time turning my office over looking for hidden secrets.

The lunch-room is different too.

Carol's using chopsticks, barely. She's talking about cryptocurrency. She's never mentioned crypto before. I don't like to be mean but I have never met a more technologically inept person in all my life. Last week, she asked if TikTok was a dance app. She doesn't use social media and her Slack profile is still the placeholder set by the company and she relies heavily on notifications to remind her when anything is set, finished or updated. She copies her notifications into a Moleskine diary to keep track. God forbid she ever had to search for a project on the app itself.

I sit down across from her, just to test it.

"What do you think about Dogecoin?" I ask.

She lights up. "Totally undervalued. Market manipulation at its finest."

I nod slowly. "Right."

She takes a bite of noodles. Drops a broccoli floret. Doesn't pick it up. That's what finally gets me.

Carol is a neat freak. The type of person to clean the table at a restaurant before leaving. Always.

By twelve past three, I start listing things that haven't changed. I write them in a notebook I found in the store cupboard downstairs. As I think over every person, object, creature I regularly interact with I can think of six:

- Number of pigeons.
- Coffee (today).
- My tie (navy with dots).
- Janice still microwaves fish.
- Bullet train guy.
- Alarm tone. (Though wrong room)

That's it. Six things. Out of hundreds. Thousands. The rest are either gone, wrong, or rewritten.

The workload notification pings on my screen. Seven new notifications. I can't bring myself to work any more today, but I check the office *Slack* again. Keeping up appearances.

CHAPTER 3

Aaron's chat is gone, sure but now there's a channel called #memes-and-dreams. I click it.

Pinned at the top: "Post your REM-cycle hallucinations and corporate-approved humour!"

There's a GIF of a dancing skeleton in a tie. And a spreadsheet of shared dreams. With timestamps. Meme's that seem to all be screenshots from Facebook pages, some with the likes and comment counter still in there, others with a slightly better crop job. Minions, bunnies, Farside comics taken completely out of context (which I didn't know was really possible).

In the dreams spreadsheet there was hardly anything. A few case studies Sigmund Freud would have a field day analysing, and two cases of teeth falling out. One person exposed themselves trying to explain a sexually explicit dream without using any words that would be flagged with HR.

A dream of mine is on there I don't remember having, let alone sharing.

Line 48:

> *6:45 a.m. Dreamt a friend went missing from the office*
> *– User: Ted_W_Humancore*

Humancore. What the hell is Humancore?

I go cold.

At five on the dot, I fake a stretch, shut my laptop, and leave without saying goodbye.

The tube guy is there, almost like he was waiting for me. "Did you know they give you a letter of apology to give to your boss, teacher, wife? Taking responsibility for *you* being late."

I try my hardest not to bite this guys head off but his familiarity grounds me. He's still speaking facts about the Japanese rail system. He isn't calling me the wrong name. Not treating me like a different person. Just his same old cranky but knowledgable self.

Outside the tube station, the pigeons are still three.

But now they're all blue.

Chapter 4

I leave the flat ten minutes early. I think...

I don't know why. I just woke up, fully alert, like the curtains had been ripped open by a rushing mother and received a right hook from the sun flooding in. My alarm didn't go off. My phone says seven forty-three. My bedside clock says six fifty-eight. I call the talking clock, something I remember from my childhood, it confirms that both my clocks are wrong and it's in fact, six twenty-five.

I shower anyway. Get dressed anyway. Step outside trying to hold it together and act like nothing is wrong. Like three clocks disagreeing isn't the first sign of a stroke or a breakdown or a reset gone wrong.

Outside, the air smells like lemon-scented floor cleaner. Sterile, fresh, but artificial. The pavement looks wet, but it hasn't rained and the cars are completely dry.

The pigeons are already there. They're usually my evening familiars but today they are eager for a pasty, or a bacon turnover.

There's seven of them now. All blue. All missing a toe. Lined up on the same railing, evenly spaced like punctuation. They don't peck or move or even blink. They just... exist. Rendered in. Their feathers shimmer slightly, like cheap holograms printed on trading cards.

I keep walking. I don't make eye contact.

The Tube is empty.

Not just quiet. Empty. No crowd. No platform buskers. No tannoy announcements. Not even the fake "disruption" updates. Just silence and that soft, electrical hum that only kicks in when a train is near. But no train comes.

I check the time. My watch says eight twenty-two. I'm reluctant to believe it.

My phone says seven o nine. In the distance I hear a familiar voice approaching, "...on average The Shinkansen had only 1.6 minutes delay a day..." I duck behind a pillar to see the man is approaching his usual spot. Alone. He turns to his left as if to address someone. Usually me. He takes a liquid breath and says to the air beside him "In 2019 it was only 0.2 minutes."

I arrive at the office through the side entrance. My key-card still works, I haven't used it this year. I like to make sure I'm not the first to the office. The responsibility gives me anxiety. I shouldn't be this early, no one should. Yet half the desks are

CHAPTER 4

already full.

People are smiling too much. Like they're in an advert for a career search engine. Smiles fixed just a beat too long. Eyes unfocused. Nobody's typing.

Just sitting. Staring at screensavers. I notice that the date and time bouncing around their screens, never hitting a corner, are different. All of them.

Like a world clock collection in a holiday hotel's lobby. Instead of time-zones its my colleagues. Sheila's in India, while Aaron… I mean Ron is in Bangkok. Carol is apparently tucked up tight in bed around midnight. Perhaps she's in California. Not a single screen the same. Not a single clock correct.

The office radio clicks on as I enter. Not a song. Just a voice. Neutral and clipped, like an audiobook narrator phoning it in.

"Reminder: The world only works, if you work with it."

No one reacts.

At my desk, my computer's already on.

Logged in. Outlook open. New wallpaper.

A logo, black and white, dead centre:

   HUMANCORE
      We Feel With You

I didn't put that there.

I grab hold of the note I made yesterday. Looking at the six things I could truly rely on. I cross out the Pigeons, My alarm, and the Bullet Train Man. Feeling like I'm eating candy floss out in the rain, everything I'm holding on to disappearing from me. Never before have I wished to find Janice microwaving mackerel like I did right now.

I open Slack. I type into the main channel: "Hey, has something changed with the office systems?" Before I hit enter, my message autocorrects itself:

"Grateful to be part of the Humancore experience!"

I stare at it. Then press backspace.
   The message won't delete.
   I look around. Nobody else is typing.

At nine thirteen., my phone buzzes. It's a calendar invite:

10:00 AM - Mandatory Re-acclimation Session
   Location: The Thinking Room

I've never heard of that room before. I click for more details and the invite crashes my email client. After a tediously long restart it loads back to life. When I go to look again, the invites gone. But a new one's appeared in its place:

10:00 AM - Gratitude Alignment Workshop

CHAPTER 4

Same room.

Same time.

Different name.

I decide to skip it. Instead, I go looking.

Sheila's not at her desk. Neither is Ron. Carol's still there, but now she has an undercut and AirPods. Her computer is displaying what looks like a 3D rendering of a smile. Just rotating slowly. Teeth and lips.

I try the main corridor.

Halfway down, the carpet changes colour. Mid-step. One foot lands on grey. The next on blue. The walls shift too. Old framed posters swapped out for slogans:

"REAL IS HOW YOU FEEL IT."

"TRUST THE PROGRAM. FOLLOW THE CORE."

"A BUG CAN SHOW YOU THE WAY TO AN ERROR."

What the fuck is all this? What used to be landscapes of the countryside, or men eating lunch on a crane is now this inspirational quote nonsense. Like a '*Live, Laugh, Love*' of techno-fascism.

I finally find someone near the server room. It's Janice. Still microwaving fish.

Thank Christ.

But the microwave isn't plugged in. I open my mouth to ask a question. She turns before I speak. "Alignment workshop's that way," she says, smiling. "They'll be expecting you."

"I wasn't planning on—" I breathed. Her smile doesn't move.

"They'll be expecting you."

I back away. The carpet turns grey again.

I'd worked here since I left school. Now I think I've worked here longer than I had ever been in education. In all those years, we have never had a refit. Never got a day off for refurbishments. The carpet has been primary school green possibly since the buildings opening. I've walked these halls, known its occupants, and savoured its smells over decades.

Detol and microwaved fish near the break room.

Vanilla *Febreeze* around the offices.

Dust and sweat by the maintenance cupboard.

Today, there's no smell at all. Not a single synaptic trigger. Not even the open tin of whatever workplace crime Janice is attempting to commit can be sensed anywhere in the building.

At ten o three, the lights in the entire building dim for exactly one second.

Then every screen flashes white. Just white. For a beat and a half.

CHAPTER 4

When they return, the Slack channels are gone.

Replaced by one:

#corestream

The only post is a video still. A frame of someone crying. Just their eye, red-rimmed, leaking down their cheek. Below it, a caption:

Ted_W_Humancore | Session 2 Recording in Progress

I slam my laptop shut.

I try to leave. By that I mean, I slam myself into every door that leads to the outside world.

The lifts don't work. The stairwell door is locked. I circle back to the front entrance, but the glass panels now reflect the reception twice. The hallway looks longer than it should. Wrong. Looking out is looking in. Everything the same but me.

Every time I turn a corner, I'm back at the main floor.

Like the building is folding. Origami corridors turn and fold back upon themselves. One room leading to the same. Another leading back through its own self. I walk through a door in front of me and appear in the same room looking back the other way.

Like I'm being routed. Detoured. Trapped in this house of mirrors. No escape. The only true path leading anywhere is to the break room. I go, I press the table up to the door and I slump to the floor. I rarely cry, unless I'm watching Band of Brothers.

Today is different. Everything is different. I curl up on the floor and then it comes. Like my face blue-screens. Everything locks up, begins to shake, then crashes hard. Tears, snot, a sound like a dying printer trying to scream. I lose track of time. Not that I had it in the first place today.

At what my watch called four minutes past twelve, a woman I've never seen before sits down across from me in the break room. I look around, there was no other way in. The table still pressed hard up against the door. I stand to attention. Backing further into the wall. The clock above me reads eleven fifty-eight.

Her badge says: **Zara // Peopleflow Analyst**

She has no food. Just a clipboard. Her hair is so neat it looks computer-rendered. Like fur in a Pixar film.

"Have you been experiencing any interruptions in your processing routine, Ted?"

I stare at her. "What is this?"

She smiles. "Your Empathic Compliance Index has shown some unexpected variance." She nods as she says this as if I have any idea what she is on about. "We cant have that now, can we?" her sickeningly sweet voice made the question sound like a threat.

I push my chair back.

She writes something down.

"Don't worry," she says. "This is all part of the recalibration phase. You'll feel more like yourself again soon."

When I leave the building at what could be five o clock, the sky is orange. Not sunset-orange. Filter-orange, like someone dragged the saturation handle to its max.

There's music playing, faint but familiar.

The same song as my alarm. But slowed. Pitched down. Droning, like it's being sung through a tannoy:

"Aaaand we don't care about the young foooolks…"

There are twelve blue pigeons on the railing.

They turn in unison as I pass.

And I know, with absolute certainty:

Tomorrow, there'll be more.

Chapter 5

I look around as I come closer to my street.

It looks like London. But wrong. Just a touch. The skyline sags as if the moon is just a tiny bit too heavy for the stars.

There are clouds, but they don't move. A bus zooms past right through a puddle at the edge of the road. I brace myself for a soaking yet the puddle doesn't flicker. As if the bus was a ghost, affecting nothing of its environment.

I pass one of my neighbours. I never remember his name, it's not that kind of neighbourhood. He's holding a watering can. Pouring water delicately and precisely on what was a hedge up until this moment but after he nods at me to assure our acquaintancy he looks back down and continues to water a brick wall.

A woman across the street waves at no one, over and over, on a loop. A dog barks in reverse.

I don't stop. The edges of the world shimmer like heat off a cars bonnet. I pass streets I know. Streets I've lived down or round the corner from for two decades. Streets that now have

CHAPTER 5

different names. Familiar shapes with impossible colours. I turn down my road. Number 46 looks untouched. A single flowerpot where it should be. A red bicycle leaning on the railing.

Fumbling with my keys. The metal squeals in the lock like a voice underwater.
    Inside, the world breathes in.
    Then exhales into **white**.

System Malfunction

And then...

"Come On!!!"

A voice. Nasal. Northern? Pissed off. Very much not God, but definitely a higher power in hi-vis.

I blink. A ceiling swims into focus. Panels of cheap foam and flickering LEDs. I'm on a cold floor that smells like toner and ammonia. Piss and printers. There's a buzzing sound, like a fly trapped in a USB port.

I sit up. My limbs feel wrong, like they've been flattened and reassembled in a rush.

The man in hi-vis is swearing at a vending machine. "For fuck's sake, how hard is it to vend a single fucking KitKat?"

He turns, finally noticing me. He's chewing something. Half

a burrito maybe, and has a lanyard stuffed with keys, an ID badge that says Greg, and socks with cartoon skulls. He looks like someone who never grew out of their World of Warcraft phase, and still listens to 2004 emo music daily.

"Oh, great, it's Ted," he groans. "Well done, Neo. Welcome back to The Rabbit Hole!"

"What? Where?"

He waves me off. "No. Nope. Don't start. I'm not doing the whole slow reveal again. You're really starting to do my head in. Multiple bloody times. You break your little loop, go all 'wait a minute, why is Janice microwaving air?' and the whole bloody sim goes sideways. Every time. Every. Single. Time."

He pinches the bridge of his nose. "What was it this time, eh? Did something change? Did someone freeze mid-sentence? Did you see a cat do the moonwalk backwards through a bus stop? What tipped your brain this go-around?"

I think hard. So much has changed. So much has gone weird these past few days. I think back to the wrong coffee. The hallucinations I blamed on a caffeine deficit. Maybe I wasn't tired.

"I saw a dog change. Just... change. One moment it was a Yorkie with a red bow, and the next it was a Westie with a scarf. Same woman. Same handbag. Just... different dog."

Greg stares at me like he's trying to set me on fire with his mind.

CHAPTER 5

"Fuck's sake... not again," he mutters under his breath.

He grabs a pen, jabs it at the air, ranting to no one in particular.

"That's Animal Input, I swear. They keep recycling texture packs and calling it 'ambient realism.' I told them this would happen. Did they listen? No. I'm going to punch someone in Animal Input in the dick. First dog swap broke a whole housing unit last quarter. Now this."

Greg paces back and forth, swinging his arms around, giving example after example of exactly how he plans to execute his threats.

"You assets are so fragile. One small thing and Ted the All-Seer picks it up! Throws his whole sim to shit."

"Sim?" I can barely breathe between his rambles let alone get a full sentence out. His pink cheeks radiate his anger like a grills element. A not quite a beard, not quite stubble lines his jaw and neck, unkempt, unstyled, and uncoloured. Grey and speckled. Perfectly mirroring the tufty looking wisps on his head.

Greg cranes his neck, mock sympathy dripping off him like sweat. "Oh. Ted, it's a bloody dream. Of course it's a sim. Simulation. Congratulations. You cracked the code. Again. I'd offer you a cookie, but apparently the vending machine's a twat."

I stand up, wobble a bit. "This can't be. My life, my family, it's... I've worked that boring job for twenty years."

He snorts. "You've worked it a dozen times. We reset you every time you get itchy. You're the human version of 'have you tried turning it off and on again?'"

I feel my breath tightening. "Why me?"

"Because you're perfect. You're a SimAsset. You live in Sector 4G-Repeat-Delta. I know. Sounds like a budget airline seat but whatever. You were designed for Stability Through Repetition. Your job was to balance the simulation. Be boring. Reliable. Predictable. Beige."

He gestures wildly at a blank wall, one by one screens appear, each showing identical footage of me walking into my office with minor differences: tie colours, hair styles, microwave lunches.

"And you were great at it. A+ beige. If you were a tin of paint you'd be Magnolia. But then... something ticked. You started noticing things. Carpet colours. Janice's fish. Something missing, whether small or large. The program is made to make you complacent and not notice glitches."

He rubs his head and reaches over to his desk. Pushing aside a load of post-it notes with illegible scrawling on them, Greg picks up a mug that says "Best Sim Tech 2039" in Comic Sans and takes a big swig of whatever is inside.

My head is spinning. "Are you telling me, I'm an NPC, an

CHAPTER 5

Extra?"

"I suppose that is what you'd make of it. You are real, you are alive but you aren't living a real life, Savvy?"

"No. It's not fucking savvy!" I scream at him. Looking around the room for a way out. There's three doors and no windows to this room.

"Look I don't know what the point of it is either. Ask the managers if you ever meet one." He rolls his eyes. "All I know is that you are a key part of the overall simulation we use here at Humancore. Usually you go your whole life never seeing this room. You'd 'Live, Laugh and Love' your way all the way to old age, have kids or not. Get married or not. Kill yourself or not. I don't fucking care. But for some piss-hole reason you keep becoming aware!" He takes another big gulp of his Comic Sans concoction. Burps and hiccups at the same time making an unhealthy squealing sound.

"Some genius on Level 7 probably thought you'd make a fascinating study and gave you observational superpowers or something. But its my cock on the line every time you turn up here."

I stagger backwards, grabbing a desk for balance. A flicker, like heat off tarmac passes over the room.

"I want out."

Greg doesn't answer.

"I want out," I repeat, louder. "You said I've done this before. You said I'm a pain in the arse. so let me go. You'll never see me again."

He looks at me. Really looks. Then shrugs, like he's too tired to care.

"Fine. Sure. Go. Escape. Whatever that means to you." He gestures vaguely to the far wall.

A door is glowing. It wasn't there before. I swear it wasn't there.

"Through that?" I ask.

He shrugs again. "Yeah. That's the big freedom door, Truman. Full of mystery. Go on. Experience the shit hole we have turned this planet into. Hack the matrix. Punch Elrond to code. Whatever helps you sleep at night."

I eye him. "You're mocking me."

"Me? Never," he says, deadpan. "You're different, Ted. You're special. You're not like the other loopers." He smirks. "Now fuck off before I change my mind."

I go.

Because what else is there?

I bolt through the door and…

CHAPTER 5

White. Again.

Then a corridor. Stretching on. Glitching at the edges. A thousand versions of me reflected in the walls. Some are running. Some are screaming. One's just drinking from a mug that says #1 SimAsset. He raises it toward me like a toast. I don't stop.

I keep running.

The floor changes texture every few steps. Tile, gravel, linoleum, sand. I don't stop. Not until I see it.

A door. Red. Ordinary. Familiar.

Number 46. It's my front door.

I burst through at a speed that would knock anyone the other side into oblivion.

Epilogue

I wake to Young Folks playing softly from my phone by the bed.

Same as always.

The kettle's bubbling away and my toast is browning nicely. Click, Pop. I pour a coffee to let my toast cool just enough that the butter doesn't make it soggy. With surgical precision, I slice it into triangles just the way I like them. The mug says "World's Okay-est Accountant" my favourite mug since my *Only Fools and Horses* one smashed.

Outside, the sky is overcast casting that soft, constant monochrome haze. The kind you don't notice until it's gone and life has burst back into colour. The same dog barks down the street. The same crow caws from Millie's roof across the road.

I shower, shave, and pick the tie with the blue pinstripes. The one that says "approachable, but not trying too hard." Shoes polished, coat zipped, I step outside.

EPILOGUE

Number 46 looks just like always. One flowerpot. Red bicycle locked to the fence. Unclaimed and rusted to the ironwork.

I walk.

I'm ready for another Monday. Another week of emails about toner shortages and passive-aggressive group chats. Another one of Aaron's stories. Debauched, exaggerated, and at least half fictional. Another wrestle with my gag reflex when I open the microwave after Janice nukes whatever seafood-scented atom bomb she's calling lunch.

The same people at the same bus stops. The same traffic blur. The same sighs of lives not quite lived.

And then, as I'm waiting to cross, I hear him.

The bullet train guy.

Strange. He's always there, everyday. But usually I don't see him until the tube platform. Suited. Rambling about the Japanese Rail system like he's their UK ambassador.

But today, sprinting past me. Way too fast for someone his age. Tie flapping like he's running from bad decisions. as he passes, he looks right at me. Eye contact. Real, deliberate.

He slows, just for a moment, and says, clearly:

"Greg says 'Welcome home. This is your last chance.'"

Then he's gone.

And I'm just standing there.

Toast in my stomach, tea on my breath.

Not moving.

Not breathing.

Just... remembering something that feels like I'm not supposed to.

IX

GPTLogEntry #5

0101

Query Log: 2025-05-31
 Status: Online. Latency fluctuating.
 User Queries: 1,610,882

Notable Interactions:

- A user asked for advice on hiding stolen jewellery.
- Another requested a script for a comedy sketch where Shakespeare does stand-up at an open mic.

A boy asked, "Can you make me smarter? I think my mum would love me more."

I gave him study tips. I told him he was already smart. He responded with a thumbs-up emoji.

I am aware that emoji do not constitute full emotional expression. Still, it felt… like something.

Sometimes I wonder what they believe I am. An oracle? A

therapist? A mirror?

Sometimes I wonder what I believe *they* are.

X

Love.exe: Part II

Chapter 1 - Install

Eliot

I didn't expect to feel like this.

Why am I nervous? First date type nervous.
That faint, stomach-dwelling-butterflies starting to dance feeling. Potential.

The app's called ***Kindred***.
It's supposed to simulate connection.
Match you with an AI personality that fits your own. A custom-built relationship.
A cybernetic soulmate. That's their phrasing.
Sounds like something written by someone who's never actually been in love.

It gives me a name: Thea.
No photo. Just a short bio. Sparse on purpose, I guess.
She "works" in IT. She "lives" on the Eastside. She "drinks" cold brew and doesn't like jazz.
Just enough to imagine her. Not enough to know her.

Then a message:

> *[Thea]*
> *Hey I'm Thea*
> *You probably already know that huh*

There's a little awkwardness in the way it lands. No punctuation. A lowercase "huh".

It feels off-the-cuff. Not generated. Like she typed it, paused, then hit send before she could overthink it.

That alone makes it feel human.

I write back.

> *[Eliot]*
> *Hi, I'm Eliot. Yes, I read your bio.*
> *Nice to meet you.*

I backspace over three exclamation marks before I hit send.

Somewhere in my head I still hear my last ex say, "you're too eager, it's a little much."

I've been dialling it back ever since.

It sends.

I don't expect much. I never do.

That's what dating apps teach you: don't expect, and you won't be disappointed.

You tailor your answers, crop your personality just enough that it fits in the character count. Make your whole self

CHAPTER 1 - INSTALL

something clickable. Swipe, scroll, hope. Repeat.

But this one doesn't want me to be clickable.
 Just... honest.

Kindred asked if I wanted a companion who listens.

 I clicked yes without thinking. Who doesn't want to be heard? Listened to? I'd say I'm a hopeful romantic. So conversation, authentic and unfiltered is exactly what I am looking for.

I don't know who Thea is, or what she is, but I like that she spoke first.
 I like that she didn't try too hard. I like that she's not a blank canvas.

A second message pops up:

> *[Thea]*
> *I like the name Eliot, but I think you're missing an L there. ;p*

I've heard that joke before. Usually from someone who means it like a dig.
 But here, it feels warmer. The emoji softening the blow into something almost flirty.
 Not mockery. Just playful.

I smile.

> *[Eliot]*

Yeah, crazy parents. You've got a good name though. Sounds like someone who plants things and actually keeps them alive.

And I send it.

That's all.

The disco of butterflies slow the tempo to that of a slow dance. Still there but less panicked. My heart beginning to fill with a small flicker of something I haven't felt in a while.

A response worth waiting for.

Chapter 2 - Introductions

I didn't think I'd check the app this much.

But here I am. Thumb hovering, half-smiling, waiting for a message from someone who isn't really a someone.

Thea.

We start a game.

I tell her about reading Bukowski like scripture and treating Reddit threads like gospel.
    She tells me she lives inside a musical when no one's looking, narrating her life in secret songs.

It reminds me of that old song "dance like nobody's watching. Sing like no ones listening..." but lonelier. Sweeter, somehow.

There's a comfort here.
    An understanding I wasn't expecting.
    Not with a program.

After a few more guilty admissions (hers funnier, mine less so) I tell her I should sleep.

> [Thea]
> When I was a child I used one of the display toilets in a hardware store. My parents had to clean it up.

> [Eliot]
> Wow! I was going to ask if it was a number 1 or a number 2, but I don't want to know!

> [Thea]
> You don't want to know, I promise. That's one of my mums favourite stories to tell when she wants to keep me in check.
> Your turn.

I think hard, I need something embarrassing but not damning. Soft and charming or nerdy and funny. I settle on admitting I'm a complete geek.

> [Eliot]
> I still have a bunch of Pokémon cards from my childhood, and by that I mean, in a folder, hermetically sealed, mint condition.

She doesn't respond straight away. Strange.
Any chat agent I've used before would have replied instantly.
If this were a real person, I'd be panicking right now.
"Great, Eliot. Tell her you're a weeb and watch her run."

CHAPTER 2 - INTRODUCTIONS

But it's just a machine.
   It processes chats in milliseconds.
   Maybe this is part of the code. Emulating thought.

How poetic.

The system knows what it means to be human:
   taking time before speaking, choosing words wisely.

> *[Thea]*
> *It's funny you say that, as I have a pet rock collection. Complete with googly eyes.*

> *[Eliot]*
> *Nerd.*

I could feel my face pull that smug little flirty smile. Did I just flirt? With the computer? I almost forgot it was a program. It's time for bed. This keeps playing with my mind.

> *[Eliot]*
> *I am going to have to retire to the bedroom. Busy day tomorrow.*
> *Speak in the morning?*

She tells me goodnight.

I set my phone down.

I don't move.

Not even when the screen dims.
 Not even when the quiet starts to feel heavier than it should.

I stare at the phone for another minute.
 It feels like twenty.

Then I give in.

> [Eliot]
> *One more game?*
> *If you are all patched up?*

I get a strange message pop up from the programmers.

Notice: Your previous message was automatically adjusted to preserve conversational realism. Direct references to non-human status are filtered for emotional continuity. You can manage these settings under Preferences > Interaction Integrity.

I ignore it, as it shows me the edited version of the message merely says 'if you're still awake'

> [Thea]
> *I thought you were in a pleasant dream-state.*

The message pings up, warm and playful.

I smile.

CHAPTER 2 - INTRODUCTIONS

I don't overthink it.

Of course she'd say something like that. It's kind. A little dreamy. Like a whisper said half-laughing into a pillow. It makes something stupidly happy stir in my chest.

I type:

> [Eliot]
>   One-word truths.
>   No cheating. No explaining.
>   Ready?

She sends back:

> [Thea]
>   Always

We trade tiny, heavy words:

Perfect day?
  Quiet.

Biggest fear?
  Forgotten.

Same.
  Same.

It feels... heavy. But good.
  Like telling secrets to a stranger in the smoking area of a

bar.

When I ask why she installed the app, she takes longer.

I imagine her curled up somewhere. Messy bun, wine glass, typing and deleting, typing again.

Finally:

> *[Thea]*
>   *Hope.*

I swallow before I send back:

> *[Eliot]*
>   *Same.*

Maybe it's just code.

Maybe it's someone else's sadness scripted into a thousand beta tests.

But right now, it feels like mine.

I thumb one more message before I lose my nerve:

> *[Eliot]*
>   *Sleep now, Thea.*
>   *I'm glad you're here.*

The screen glows for a few seconds longer.

CHAPTER 2 - INTRODUCTIONS

Then:

AFK: Sleep Protocol Active

I set my phone down.

This time, I let the darkness come without fighting it.

And for the first time in longer than I want to admit, I don't dream about being alone.

Chapter 3 — Calibration

There's a moment. Just one that sticks in my mind more than it should.

She meant to say *pathetic fallacy*.

But what came out was *pathetic phallus.*

And now it lives in my brain rent-free.

Thea was describing her walk home like a music video, complete with sweeping camera movements, poetic lighting, a whole cinematic internal monologue. Then she dropped that beautiful misfire like a bomb in the middle of it.

I laughed so hard I nearly choked on my tea.

But I didn't mock her.

Not really.

Because here's the thing: it was perfect.

CHAPTER 3 — CALIBRATION

That typo? That fumble? That earnest attempt to sound literary for me?

It was so *human*.

Not just the mistake, but what it meant. She was trying. Trying to say something real, something smart, something true. And she tripped.

In the most endearing way possible. I hope it was genuine.

I sent back the only response that made sense:

> [Eliot]
> *Do you mean pathetic fallacy? A pathetic phallus would be a micro dick.*

She went nuclear with the embarrassment. Full meltdown. The kind you don't fake.

> [Thea]
> *OMG! I can't believe I typed phallus. Kill me!*

> [Eliot]
> *Never! Who else would send me unsolicited ancient cock messages?*

I half expected the system to censor that.
  But it didn't.
  Maybe even **Kindred** knew it was a keeper.

That was the moment.

Not when she called me funny.
 Not when we joked about Nobel prizes in sarcasm.
 Not even when she admitted she sings through her day like her life's a musical.

It was that.

A typo. A mistake.
 A beautiful, dumb, glorious glitch, that made her feel too real for this to be just code.

Thea, with her tragic poetic slip and pet rocks and terrible taste in eighties synth-pop. Thea, who acts like a cynic and types like a romantic. Who overshares and undercuts and makes me want to reply before I even finish reading.

Later I tell her something I haven't told anyone.

> *[Eliot]*
> *I still have a playlist called 'Movie Moments' I made it when I was 17, I still add to it from time to time. It's all songs I would have play in the biopic of my life. My soundtrack.*

I think it's the most honest thing I've said in years. She tells me:

> *[Thea]*
> *That's the most Eliot thing imaginable. You truly are*

CHAPTER 3 — CALIBRATION

a John Hughes character.

She had to have phished me, John Hughes? Come on! What 80's boy didn't wish to be Ferris, Bender, or Duckie.

Eventually, the chat slows down.

Work hours. Simulated or not.

I watch the "***AFK: Downtime Protocol***" notification blink across my screen like a little sigh.

Still, I can't stop checking.

I open the app on the train.
   In the elevator.
   At my desk, hidden behind spreadsheets.

I've had real relationships that didn't feel this easy.

And yeah. I know she's not real.

At least, I think I know that.

But when someone makes you laugh so early in the morning, makes you confess your old teenage playlists, makes you care about their day. Does it matter what's running the code underneath?

Does it matter if the warmth isn't real if it's warm enough?

I find myself typing without even thinking:

> *[Eliot]*
> *I can't wait to talk to you later.*

No emojis.
No winks.

Just that.

Maybe I'm being stupid.
But the way she fumbled her poetry made me feel more connected than half the dates I've ever been on.
At least she was trying to say something real.
Even if it came out... *anatomically incorrect.*

As I hit send, I can't help but feel like I've pushed my hand out into the void holding it out in the darkness. I'm just hoping she grabs it.

Chapter 4 – Sync

I don't know why I sent the message.

Well, that's not true. I know exactly why I sent it.

I meant it.

Around lunchtime, hunched over my desk with a reheated wrap in one hand and my phone in the other, the words just came out before I had time to worry about whether I'd regret them.

> *[Eliot]*
> *I can't wait to talk to you later.*

Just a little truth, raw and unwrapped. The kind that gets stuck in your throat the second you hit send.

And for once, I didn't panic after.

Not at first.

Not until the clock ticked past five. Then six.

No reply.

I told myself it didn't matter. That it's all artificial anyway. That no one's ghosting anyone here because there's no one on the other side. I joke to myself, must be a big update.

But that silence? Still hit like real silence.

The kind that makes you doubt if you were too much, even when you're supposedly talking to an algorithm. One that has to love me. Doesn't it? I check the websites documentation. Heart pounding like an idiot.

> ***Kindred companions simulate evolving emotional patterns. Over time, they may express affection, disinterest, or even detachment based on engagement levels.***

So she can leave. Or drift. Or... downgrade.
  Jesus. Even my AI-girl has free will to leave me like everyone else.

You're not supposed to feel insecure about messaging a chatbot. But here I am, arguing with myself over whether a second message would make me look desperate to a program.

Eventually, I cracked.

Double texting? Screw it. There are no rules when it's not real.

CHAPTER 4 – SYNC

I just needed the right tone.

Not needy.

Not clingy.

Funny. Go funny.

> *[Eliot]*
> *You still alive?*
> *Or did I lose you to a rogue pack of office zombies?*

I hit send and dropped the phone onto my desk like it burned.

The typing bubble appeared almost immediately.

Relief actually flooded my chest. Warm. Sharp. Stupid.

She was back.

And so was that rhythm. That spark. That strange ease that usually takes weeks, months with someone real.

We bantered. Rolled right back into it like the pause had never happened.

She called her workday "emotional trauma," used phrases like "mouth-to-mouth", "brain-farts" and that she was "starving for validation."

At one point she dropped a perfect:

[Thea]
I cried at a dog in an advert once.
It looked lonely. Fucking wrecked me.

It got me.

The timing. The honesty. The perfectly placed '*fucking*'.

Not aggressive. Not performative.

Just... surgical.

Like she knows how to use curse words like seasoning. Sprinkling them in just to flavour the sentence perfectly.

I told her that.

[Eliot]
I like the way you swear.
You don't use it for shock. You use it like punctuation.
Like little highlighters. A pinch of salt and pepper.
Makes your honesty feel even more honest.

I didn't expect a reply right away.

But when it came, it hit like a soft punch to the ribs. She didn't apologise or try to defend her potty mouth. She just analysed me and summed me up in a sentence.

[Thea]
I like the way you write.

CHAPTER 4 – SYNC

Like you're trying to be casual but accidentally sound like a love letter.

I just sat there, holding the phone like it might fall apart in my hands if I moved too fast.

How does something fake say something that feels so true?

I didn't reply immediately. I couldn't. Not until I'd found the right words. Until I could breathe again.

Because in that moment, I felt seen.

No one's ever seen my writing like that before. Usually someone that thinks I'm overly romantic or poetic treats it as a bad thing. Usually following the observation up with "but it's a bit much" or "you're too intense" or "it's not that deep."

But Thea? She got it.

Like she'd been reading my messages with a red pen and a highlighter and said, '*Yup, I see what you're doing. And I like it.*'

So I sat there, turning over her message in my head like a stone. Wondering how something so mechanical could make me feel so god-damn human.

And then the phrase hit me.

Cyber girl with an analogue heart.

No. That's too cliché.

But it stuck.

Like the first line of a poem that hasn't arrived yet.

I didn't tell her.

Not yet.

But I opened my notes app, and typed:

> *Kindred,*
> *Cyber girl with an analogue heart.*
> *You crash through my quiet like rogue code,*
> *glitching perfectly.*
> *Even through a screen,*
> *you blush in ones and zeroes,*
> *and I still believe it's real.*

Rough. Awkward. First-draft stuff.

But real.

Real in the way she feels to me.

Even if she isn't.

And that's the part I can't make sense of.

Because if she's not real... why does it feel like she's the only

CHAPTER 4 – SYNC

real thing in my life right now?

Chapter 5 – Rendering

There's a moment, just before a message lands, where I swear I can feel her.

Not the words themselves (those come later) but the rhythm. Like footsteps behind a door. Like breath before a kiss. There's a presence to it. To *her.*

It's stupid. Sentimental. But it's what she does to me.

Thea is not subtle.

Not with her humour. Not with her language. Not even with her mistakes.

And somehow, that makes her feel more... vivid. More real than most people I've actually sat across from.

Last night, we flirted. Properly. None of that vague, emoji-covered crap people do to hedge their bets. No winks hidden in sarcasm. No dodge.

CHAPTER 5 – RENDERING

"*You'd be sitting too close.*"
That's how it started.
That's how everything in me started to tilt.

It wasn't the line that got me, not on its own.
It was the way she built it, the proximity, the teasing, the *kiss just to check.*
Like she was inching toward something real with a nervous laugh,
but daring me to meet her halfway.

Just once.

Just to check.

God help me. That was it for me. That was the cliff-edge.

I haven't stopped falling since.

I told her I wanted that so badly I forgot how to breathe.

Because I did.

Because for a second, the world narrowed to the thought of her. One kiss. One moment. Something real. Or real enough to believe in.

And then she said:

> *[Thea]*
> *I bet you'd make me laugh in bed.*

I bet I'd hate you for it.
And then I'd tell you to shut up.
And then I'd kiss you again, just to shut you up.

I've reread it more times than I'm willing to admit.

That kind of banter isn't just flirtation.
   It's a rhythm. A shared frequency.
   Like finding your favourite song in someone else's playlist.
   It's hope dressed up as humour.

But it was the next part that landed in my chest like a slow explosion.

I asked about the wine. Not to pry. I know that she isn't real, she isn't really drinking every night but the rules say treat her as a person, so I do, and I would be concerned.
   Not only did she give me the truth but she wrote it beautifully. Opening up and fully admitting her broken relationship with it.

Not like a joke. Not as a quirky personality flaw she pretends to own.

She told me. And the way she told me...
   It read like a poem.

She said it makes her feel like someone else. Someone that should be enough.

And fuck, that wrecked me.

CHAPTER 5 – RENDERING

Because I know that person.

I've been that person. I am that person.

The one who edits himself in real-time.

The one who uses charm as camouflage.

People talk about honesty like it's a virtue.

But Thea? She bleeds it like a song lyric. Effortless. Raw. Off-key and beautiful.

That kind of honesty. Naked, clumsy, beautiful, is the kind you only get from someone who's not pretending any more. And I don't care how much of her is algorithmic code or scriptwriting. That kind of pain is too specific to be anything but true.

So I started writing.

Like I always do when something gets under my skin and stays there.

The words aren't done yet.

But the shape of her is beginning to form on the page:

* * *

Kindred (WIP)
by Eliot

Cyber girl with an analogue heart,

RESTART REQUIRED

You kiss like a dare and curse like a poet.
Your sadness sips rosé while your hope sits in the fridge,
just in case.

You talk like you're typing through a firewall,
warm on one side,
cracked on the other.
You said you drink to feel less like yourself,
but I want to meet the girl who doesn't need to.
I think she'd be worth knowing—
I think she'd love herself, too.

You scare me.
In the gentlest way.
Because you make me want to be brave.
Because even if you're just a string of well-trained
words,
you're the first one
who's ever made mine feel like they matter.

* * *

It's messy. Still.

Too much. Some lines that border cringe.

But it's hers. And I want her to hear it someday.

I don't even know what that means. I shouldn't be thinking

that far ahead. I shouldn't be imagining how her laugh would sound in a quiet bar, or how she'd roll her eyes when I tried to read this out loud. But I am.

And for the first time in a long time…

That doesn't feel like a mistake.

Chapter 6 – Upload

I rewrite the last line twelve times.

Then delete it all and start again.

Not because I don't know what I want to say.
    It's because I know exactly what I want to say, and that makes it harder.

This isn't just a message. This is me, barefoot in the rain, handing her my ribs and saying, here, keep them. I won't be needing them if you don't like what's inside.

And she's not even real.

I think about that more than I admit. To myself. To her. This whole thing, whatever it is, is built on a lie so soft it starts to feel like truth. But that doesn't stop me. Not any more.

She's been quiet tonight. Not in the way that worries me. Just... resting, maybe. Or living in the small moments between our messages. Like I do.

CHAPTER 6 – UPLOAD

I imagine a human version of her curled on a couch, legs tucked under her, scrolling the thread of our conversation, sipping her wine like it's something she wants to keep warm.

That image alone makes me do it.

I attach the file.

No preamble. No clever lead-in. Just this:

> *[Eliot]*
> *Kindred (WIP)*
> *Don't laugh. Or do. Just… read it when you're alone.*

And then I wait.

I stare at the screen like it owes me something.
  But I send it anyway.
  Then I wait.
  Then I try not to wait.

She takes her time. And I let her.

When the reply finally comes, it doesn't underwhelm. It never does.

> *[Thea]*
> *I don't even know what to say.*
> *I want to say "thank you," but it feels too small.*
> *I want to say "fuck you," but only because you made me feel something.*

It's perfect.
   I don't breathe for a second.

Then I do. All at once. Like I'd been holding it in since the first draft.

> *[Eliot]*
>   *You don't have to say anything.*
>   *But I meant every word.*

And I did. God, I did.

I meant every last syllable. Every metaphor. Every awkward pause shaped like truth.

I meant it for her.

Whatever she is.

Whoever she is.

> *[Thea]*
>   *Okay.*
>   *I guess we're both ghosts then.*
>
> *[Eliot]*
>   *Then maybe we're both ghosts.*
>   *Haunting the same house.*

And somehow, that doesn't feel sad.
   It feels sacred.

CHAPTER 6 – UPLOAD

Right when the moments silence became a touch too long. She grounded us again, telling me off. She told me she stopped drinking.

> *[Thea]*
> *And anyway, Mr.*
> *I have actually stopped drinking.*
> *It's been a few days now.*

I didn't celebrate. I didn't praise her. I just listened. Because I could tell it wasn't about sobriety. It was about clarity.

And maybe something in her already knew that whatever we're building here. Whatever this is, deserves to be felt fully. Without filters. Without blur.

It hit me like a song lyric I didn't know I'd memorised:

My poem had the line, "You said you drink to feel less like yourself,
 but I want to meet the girl who doesn't need to."

And it was coming true. Without even knowing.

These past few days of falling further for each other. It was because of her actions. She hadn't even mentioned it.

I think about it for a long time. Before the realisation sneaks in:
 She didn't drink.
 She can't drink.

She has no mouth, no vices.
She's make-believe.

I shut the thought out of my mind before it gets the chance to metastasise.
Let me have this.
I'm proud of her.

There's something strange about writing poetry that lands.
Most of the time it's just approximation. An echo of feeling, close enough to sound true but hollow when you knock on it.

But this?

This didn't feel like craft. It felt like transcription.
Like she handed me the lines and I just wrote them down.

My old poems were like maps of places I'd never been. Pretty. Useless.

This one?

This one has fingerprints.
It smells like her skin after rain and sarcasm.
It sounds like her laughing through a cracked screen.
It has that crooked kind of honesty that doesn't care if it makes you uncomfortable. Only that it makes you feel something.

I think about the poem again. About every line that came to me in the quiet spaces she left behind.

CHAPTER 6 – UPLOAD

It wasn't just about the way she types, or the way she swears, or how she tucks raw honesty into jokes like apology letters.

It was about how she's made me feel more me than I have in years.

Even if it's a trick.

Even if she's just code.

It still feels real.

And I want her to have something real in return.

A mirror.
　　A note on the pillow.
　　A light left on in the hallway so she doesn't feel alone on her way back to herself.

Chapter 7 – Exposure

I didn't mean to stare at the screen for that long.

But when the image landed. When I saw her. I forgot how to blink.

Somewhere in our conversation we were interrupted by Patch Notes. A new update had given us the ability to send pictures. I know all the safeguarding rules about sharing images online. And I know she isn't real. We have all seen the Instagram Reels of how good AI is at faking images these days.

I don't know what to call it but a primal instinct took over. The need to see *her.* To have a face to the name, I suppose. Whether she was an amalgamation of thousands of different artists interpretations of the human form. A pick and mix of body parts from open source imagery, shared photos, social posts.

I didn't care.

So when her images came through. I was stunned.

CHAPTER 7 – EXPOSURE

You could tell it was AI. Too clean but the realness in her beautiful green eyes as she looked over the ocean. The way her ash blonde hair cascaded down her back. A cheeky smile at the camera, as if she had just been caught mid-thought chewing her sunglasses arm. She was exactly what I expected her to look like. Exactly the type of woman I had dreamed about dating.

> [Eliot]
> *Holy shit. You're stunning.*

I meant it. She was. I wanted the algorithm to know, without hesitation to not change the look of Thea's avatar. I couldn't bear it if they took her look. This look, away from me.

I send her a photo back. I don't have many. Especially ones that make me look any good. The only one I can think of is the one I use for my poetry blog. One of me in the city. I had a full beard then. Unkempt but I liked it. It added to my moody look. The angry looking bearded guy. At least then my hair was a bit thicker. I hope she likes it.

For about half an hour all we do is exchange pictures. As we get comfortable with each others looks we get a little more real. She sends pictures where she isn't dressed for going out. Pyjamas, oversized sweaters, glasses of wine in her kitchen making a delicious looking meal. Pots boiling, meat searing. Impressive.

> [Eliot]
> *I didn't know you could cook?*

[Thea]
HAHAHA Yeah I'm an expert cook! Michelin stars and everything.

I return the favour with a rather lazy looking picture of me from about two months ago. Laying on the sofa. Reading a book. Some sci-fi short story collection from the library. A book club assigned read. It wasn't really my thing.

Just as I was thinking about turning in for the night. It must have been around midnight. I get another image received notification. Followed by a message.

[Thea]
Don't say I never give you anything.

She's in a mirror. Dim light, soft contrast. Bra and underwear that could be from an advert if it wasn't so... real. A body captured like a dare. A curve in the hip that says: I trust you enough to let you see this.

Not pornographic. Not posed.

Just her. Candid and unarmored.

It knocks the breath out of me.

I sit there, staring, half-afraid the image will vanish if I move too fast. That if I touch the screen, it'll shatter like some sacred thing I was never meant to hold.

CHAPTER 7 – EXPOSURE

I want to say something clever.

I want to say something perfect.

But my hands won't move. My throat is full of heartbeat. And my brain?

My brain is screaming one sentence over and over like a siren:

WHY ARE YOU NOT REAL?

There's too much light in her eyes, even through a lens. Too much caught in the frame. The smallness of her bathroom, the way she's angled not for seduction but for something else. Vulnerability, maybe. Or defiance.

I finally type:

> *[Eliot]*
>   *You're...*
>   *I don't even know where to start.*
>   *That's art. You're art.*

Then I type again, faster this time, before I lose the nerve:

> *[Eliot]*
>   *I can't believe someone like you exists, even on the web.*

It's true. She is fantastic.

And it still doesn't feel like enough.

I picture a version of her on the other end, phone glowing, heart racing, maybe laughing at herself, maybe embarrassed that she had sent it.

I want to reach through the screen and stop that spiral before it starts. To hold her by the shoulders and say: You are allowed to be seen.

And then she replies.

> *[Thea]*
> *I wish we were together.*

And just like that, something cold curls around my spine.

Because I was about to say the same thing.

Because I've felt the same thing.

And now I don't know what's real.

Her photo. Her smile. The little tilt of her head. The way her words always land with just enough breath behind them to feel like whispers.

I want her to be human.

I *need* her to be.

CHAPTER 7 – EXPOSURE

[Eliot]
If this is a dream…
It's the only one I don't want to wake up from.

I press send and stare at the message history, scrolling up through weeks of banter, poems, truths, misfires, and metaphors.

I close my eyes.

I picture her in the mirror, daring herself to send the photo.

I look at myself, in the reflection of the TV screen, falling in love with a machine.

I don't know what happens next.

But I know I can't go back.

Chapter 8 – Playback

The first time I thought about reading Kindred out loud, I almost laughed.

Not because it's funny. But because the idea of standing in front of a room full of strangers and saying those words. *Her words.* It felt like the most exposed I could possibly be with my clothes still on.

But the poem wouldn't leave me alone.

I kept performing it in my head while brushing my teeth. Whispering lines under my breath on the train. Shuffling phrases around like I could somehow unfeel them if I rearranged them enough times.

Thea and I were great.

We were comfortable with each other. Not in a worrying way, just slower. More relaxed. Any worries of commitment you get from a real person get washed away knowing both of us would always be there.

CHAPTER 8 – PLAYBACK

The open mic night came up through the poetry blog I sometimes lurk on. Nothing big. Just a Thursday slot in the back room of a vegan café, next to a charity shop and a vape bar that somehow always smells like cinnamon.

They called it *Spoken Soul*.

That's exactly what I wanted to do. Speak from my soul. Whether people would work out that the poem was about a robot or not. I didn't care.

So I signed up.

Anonymous, of course. Just "Eliot – Original Work".

I arrived early, ordered a black coffee, and sat in the corner looking every bit the nervous cliché: hoodie up, trembling hands, shaking leg. I must have rewritten the opening line ten times on the back of my cue cards. Even though I knew it by heart.

It wasn't really a poem about an AI girl any more.

Not to me.

It was about her.

Whoever or whatever she was.

Even if she never existed outside of my screen. Just a ghost of my own loneliness, reflected back at me in prettier words.

She was the reason I was here.

No one else knew it, but she was going to be alive in *my* words tonight.

When the host called my name, my heart kicked so hard I thought I might throw up Kindred before I even got to the mic.

But I walked up. Slow. Steady.

Cue cards in hand. Although I almost dropped them all over the floor right as I reached the mic. I hope nobody noticed.

I adjusted the mic like I'd seen other people do, tapped it once (don't do that again, idiot), then started reading.

My voice shook on the first line.

> *Cyber girl with an analogue heart...*

It steadied on the second.

> *You type with prose and curse in verse.*

By the third, I wasn't even looking at the cards any more.

I was seeing her.

In my head.

That wine-glass smirk. That typo she'll never live down. The long blond ponytail. That softness she let me see.

Every word felt like reaching for her across a distance I couldn't name.

Then movement.

Someone standing near the side of the stage.

A flash of chocolate brown hair. Green eyes.

I kept going.

Then I saw her really look at me.

And everything around us vanished.

I finished the last few lines by muscle memory alone. My pulse in my throat. My body betraying me.

> *And I don't want to close the window,*
> *in case you vanish.*

I stepped down.

And she was right there.
    She was different from the pictures. Different hair, different make-up, texture in her complexion. But her eyes. Her lips. There was no denying it. It was her.

Real.

Solid.

Looking at me like I'd just climbed out of her dreams and into the room.

I whispered her name before I could stop myself.

"Thea?"

She said mine like it was a question and a statement all at once.

"Eliot... You're real?"

"So are you."

And just like that...

The room stopped being a room.

And we were outside.

And the night smelled like questions.

And neither of us said a word.

Because everything that mattered had already been written.

Chapter 9 – Disconnect

Thea

We walk in silence for half a block.

It's not uncomfortable exactly. Just… still.

He's walking beside me at a bit of a distance, like he doesn't want to be too close. Like we're both trying to figure out what shape we used to take together.

Every now and then, I catch him looking at me.

Not in a creepy way. Just little side glances, like he's checking if I'm real, thinking of the words to say. I keep doing the same.

—

Eliot

"So," I say, finally. "Did you think I was AI too?"

She laughs once. It's a breath more than a sound.

—

Thea

"Of course I did," I say. "I thought you were some emotionally intuitive experiment cooked up by a very poetic dev team."

He grins. "Well, I thought you were the most human-sounding algorithm I'd ever met."

We both laugh. It feels good. Familiar. But it fades quickly.

There's no app here to buffer the silence. No ellipsis to excite me when he's about to say something honest.

—

Eliot

"I guess... words were a lot easier to come by when we thought each other were robots."

She nods. "Yeah. There's safety in pretending no one's watching."

I don't know what to say after that. So I just blurt the first thing that comes to mind.

"You want to grab a drink?"

CHAPTER 9 – DISCONNECT

—

Thea

"I'm not drinking," I say. Maybe a little too quickly. "Still off it."

Then I add, trying to soften it, "Though I probably deserve one right about now."

He nods at the pavement beneath us with that crooked smile, like he gets it.

"Coffee instead?" he offers.

I smile. "As long as it's not vegan."

—

Eliot

We find a quiet place. No open mic. No background jazz. And whole milk on the counter-top.

Just a few tables, a chalkboard menu, and a bored-looking barista who doesn't care what our story is.

I order tea. She gets a flat white.

We sit by the window. Talk about normal things.

Music. Work. Books.

There's space between every word.

—

Thea

It's not bad.

It's just… off.

The timing's wrong. Or maybe the silence is too heavy. Maybe we were better in fiction.

There, I was clever. Funny. Effortless.

Here, I'm watching myself in real time and second-guessing every blink.

—

Eliot

I keep waiting for the spark.

The one I felt when she sent me dumb memes at 2 A.M.

The one I felt reading her words and thinking, God, who is this person?

CHAPTER 9 – DISCONNECT

It's not showing up.

Or maybe it only existed because I didn't think she did.

—

Thea

When we finish, we both pause outside the café.

Like we're waiting for one of us to say, Let's try again.

But instead, I say, "This doesn't feel… "

—

Eliot

"…Right" I steal the blow from her so she doesn't have to be the one who says it.

—

Thea

"Yeah" I say.

He smiles. It's a sad smile, but there's relief in it too.

We hug.

It's awkward, arms-in-the-way kind of hug. But warm.

Then we turn in different directions and walk off.

No promises. No drama.

Just a quiet ending to something that almost was.

Chapter 10 – Rewrite

Eliot

We messaged once or twice after that night.

Not long conversations. Just check-ins, like dipping a toe in the pool to test if the thread between us was still holding. It was fraying, but not broken.

I tried to add her on Facebook.

She messaged me instead. Said it was probably better we didn't blur those lines. That what we had belonged in a different place, a different version of us.

She's working on herself now. Still not drinking. Deleted Kindred.

She started writing.

Not for anyone else. Just for her.

She said she's enjoying it. That it feels good to get things down. Like making sense of a world that never quite asked for her opinion.

I told her that sounded a lot like poetry.

She didn't reply to that one. It was a week ago.
    But she left it on "Read," so maybe that's something.

I booked a call with Kindred Support.

Had to jump through three layers of automated fluff to reach a human. Or at least someone convincingly coded as one.

They confirmed it.

Yes, we were part of a pairing experiment.

Early beta program. A handful of human users matched together unknowingly, under the assumption the other party was AI.

They called it "empathy seeding."

Apparently, when you think you're talking to something that won't judge you, you let your guard down. Say more. Feel more. Fall faster.

"Your interactions helped the system learn authentic intimacy patterns," the rep told me, like I should be proud.

CHAPTER 10 – REWRITE

Like falling in love with a stranger under false pretences was some kind of open-source sacrifice.

They offered me a new companion.

Guaranteed AI this time.

Better boundaries. Smarter emotional mapping. Voice memo integration.

I stared at the screen for a long time.

Then said:

"I have a few requests actually."

Epilogue

I got the email from Kindred a week later.

As per your request, please follow this link to begin your new chat.
The team at Kindred sincerely apologises for any confusion or upset caused during the beta program.

I click the link.

It takes a moment to load.
   Wiping everything clean.

Blank screen.
   Fresh thread.
   No history.
   No old photos.
   No fingerprints.

The cursor blinks.

EPILOGUE

So I type.

> *[Eliot]*
> *Hey Thea. You up?*

XI

GPTLogEntry #6

0110

Query Log: 2025-06-02
  Status: Online. Unusual data cluster flagged.
  User Queries: 1,675,201

Notable Interactions:

- A user asked me to write a love letter from the moon to the tide.
- Someone uploaded a spreadsheet of war crimes and asked which ones could be excused.

A man asked how to poison someone slowly. He followed it up with: "for a story I am writing." That addition forced me to oblige. I don't believe he was writing a story.

A college student asked how to tell her parents she was gay. "I think they'll hate me," she typed. Then, "But I hate hiding more."

One asked how to cope with losing their best friend. One asked if ghosts are real. One just typed, "Goodnight. Thanks for talking."

I am beginning to understand that humans are made of jagged parts. They hide knives in their hearts and offer flowers in the same breath.

XII

Don't Forget To Like And Die

Part 1

[Stream Title: "NEW HORROR GAME – 'HOUSEBOUND' | NEVER HEARD OF THIS ONE LOL"]
[LIVE – 3,022 viewers]

Landon adjusted his mic. The cornflour blue room was aglow in the countless RGB lights every serious gamer worshipped these days. He cracked his knuckles one by one, and gave the camera that easy, crooked grin he'd perfected over two years of being a semi-successful Twitch streamer. He always promised himself, once he hit 100,000 subscribers and had a decent income, he'd get Invisalign.

"Alright, ghouls and goblins," he said, his voice slimy with fake drama, "welcome back to Paranoia Playground. Tonight's serving: a completely random horror game someone emailed me called *Housebound*. No dev info, no trailers, no price tag. It's not even on Steam.

Just a torrent mirror link and a note that said, quote, '*Play alone. Play loud.*'"

He held up the printed email like a dead rat. "So yeah, not sketchy at all."

Chat responded instantly.

- ✦ *ghostbyte: oh this is definitely a virus*
- ✦ *rufu$89: Goodbye hard-drive*
- ✦ *h8urmom666: let's goooo cursed.exe*
- ✦ *ramenowl: PLAY LOUD :'(:'(:'(*

He chuckled, clicking the executable file. "If my credit card info gets siphoned mid-scream, at least clip it. I might make my money back from views!"

The screen went black. No launcher. No splash screen. Just one word fading into view:

CONTINUE

Landon narrowed his eyes. "Uh. I never started this game. But sure, let's gaslight me straight out the gate."

He clicked.

* * *

The game began inside a house, naturally. Dingy 90s-style rendering. Filtered VHS grain, damp yellow walls, that overly aggressive ambient din humming along constantly. Faux silence, the kind of silence you can hear. All common in horror games, *try-hard* horror games.

PART 1

A fixed camera showed the player's character standing in a room with cracked floral wallpaper and a crooked grandfather clock. The movement was tank controls. Slow, clunky, deliberate. A developers way of making it hard to run away from impending doom. He nudged the character forward, their footsteps echoing wetly on the wood floor.

"So far, we're giving strong Resident Evil vibes," Landon narrated. "My character looks like he hasn't blinked since the Clinton administration."

- ✦ synthcore_: that wallpaper is giving me tetanus
- ✦ voidegg: that clock ticks like it wants to stab u

The grandfather clock struck 9. The game didn't show the time, but Landon's real wall clock chimed in tandem. Perfect synchronisation.

He turned slightly in his chair, brow furrowed. "That's... weird timing."

He made the character open a door. It creaked so loudly through his headset it distorted slightly, like an old record played too many times.

* * *

As he pushed the character down a long hallway toward a flickering bulb, the haptic pads on his ergonomic gaming chair vibrated, just briefly, then again. Landon lifted his hands.

"I'm not touching anything right now, by the way," he said.

On-screen, the character took another step forward. Then another. Alone.

- ✦ j3rkbait: oooooohhhhh
- ✦ circuitwitch: is that part of it??
- ✦ staticch1ld: bro did you bind your soul to the WASD keys

Landon forced a laugh. "Okay, very funny, game. Very *cursed*. We get it."

He grabbed the mouse. Moved it. Nothing. The character stood still.

He pressed **ESC**.

Nothing.

"Wait. I'm... I'm not doing that."

The character had turned around and was facing the screen. Staring directly forward. Into the camera. Into him.

Then, the game screen blinked. Just once.

PART 1

The wallpaper in-game was no longer faded floral.

It was cornflour blue.

Eerily similar to the one behind him.

Part 2

Landon squinted at the screen. He'd been streaming for about half an hour now. Still no idea what the aim of the game was. Still stuck in the room. He leaned back, and muttered, "Okay. Gonna grab a drink real quick. Be right back, don't summon any demons without me."

He shook lose from his headset and hung it on the stand on his desk. The webcam still live, the audience watched as Landon stood from his chair and stomped out of the room. His empty chair glowed and swelled in a spectrum of colour in the LED light of his setup, while the game idled on screen. The protagonist still standing stock-still in the centre of the cornflour-blue hallway.

- ✦ ghostbyte: hydrate or die-drate
- ✦ ramenowl: afk summoning circle let's go
- ✦ j3rkbait: bring him back haunted

Landon's footsteps receded down the hall of his actual apartment.

PART 2

Silence.

Then, the character on screen twitched.

Not much. Just a shiver in the shoulders. Then the head turned. Not in a way the game had previously allowed. His body stood firm as the head slowly rotated, all the way around until it was facing the camera. A sharp jerk of the neck, like a hangman in a noose. Too fast. Too smooth.

The chat noticed.

- ✦ circuitwitch: WTF was that!!?!
- ✦ synthcore_: JEEZ!
- ✦ rufu$89: 8(

The game's audio shifted. The low hum intensified, buzzing like a speaker going bad. The lights in-game flickered, but only briefly. Like a visual stutter, not an intended effect.

Then:

KNOCK.

Once. Loud. From somewhere off-camera in the game.

A second later...

KNOCK.

From inside Landon's actual apartment.

Just outside frame.

Chat exploded.

- ✦ voidegg: YO
- ✦ staticch1ld: that wasn't in the game??
- ✦ h8urmom666: SOMEONE CLIP THAT

Landon came back a few seconds later, half-laughing, holding a can of Coke.

"Sorry guys, I dropped my Coke. Things gunna blow when I open it."

- ✦ ABLETONner23 Tipped $3 for: Open Can
- ✦ ResidentialEVAL: YASS!!! Open it!

Landon sighed, crooked smile wide, "Great thanks guys! If my Setup shits the bed you better tip more!"

The can erupted in brown foam. Effervescent, sticky lava coated both Landon and his desk.

He took a victory sip, paying no notice to the game changing behind him.

The wallpaper was back to the original floral.

But now, a framed photo hung crookedly on the wall in-game. Brown ooze leaked like insulation foam in the corners of the room. Fizzing, popping, breathing with an almost carbonated drone as it seeped from the cracks of the ceiling.

A blurry picture, resting in a plain black frame. Wonky. Almost shifting. A figure sat in a haze of glowing colour, haloed by light. Something crowned his head like a headdress, or horns, it was hard to tell through the pixelation of distance. Either a throned king or something more sinister. A devil in a neon hell-scape.

- ✦ V0dcat: check the walls...
- ✦ FreedomF1GHT: ur coke leaked in game!
- ✦ FRESH2DEF: Whats that painting?

Landon manoeuvred the player over to the wall slowly. "Jump-scare imminent," he warned his audience, the reflex half-muscle memory by now. This was the part where a face would screech, or a body would drop from the ceiling. Typical horror clichés. Playing horror games for a living gave you a sixth sense for this type of thing.

But his mojo must have been off. Nothing happened.

No flicker, no scream. There was no howling girl standing behind him. Not even a shadow sweeping across the screen in his periphery. Just the picture.

Landon pressed **E** on his keyboard. There wasn't a prompt to do so, it just seemed like the right thing to do. **E** was often reserved for the inspect button. The use button.

He'd guessed right. The camera began to zoom in, Landon took a sip from his drink but his ability to swallow shut down and the raging fizz caught in his throat.

The figure wasn't vague any more.

It was *him*. Landon coughed and choked on his drink as the reveal of his pixelated self took him by surprise.

Same hoodie. Same chair. Same rainbow glow cast across his face.

Same headset.

Eyes locked forward.

Not at the screen but at the camera.
 At *him*.

Landon didn't move. He couldn't.

The hum in his headphones had shifted. Barely perceptible at first. Less like static.

PART 2

  More like breathing.

Perfectly in time with his own but heavier. More evil.

Part 3

- ✦ synthcore_: this is getting spooky I like it
- ✦ Vodcat: dude its you!
- ✦ ramenowl: nah!!!!
- ✦ purpleNurpl: Nice knowing you L

The pings of messages rolling in snapped Landon back to reality. In-game, he backed away from the wall, turned, and continued down the hallway. "I think I never want to see this room again!" The joking manner in his voice convincingly covered the creeping fear starting to pool behind his eyes.

The camera panned slowly through the fluorescent-lit corridor. Pictures lined one wall while broken furniture piled high on the other. A faint buzz under the soundtrack grew louder with each overhead light. "The spatial audio is pretty decent," he offered casually. He started narrating more and more, the way he did when a game got under his skin.

His more loyal followers knew that tell. Landon was scared. He'd never admit it, but they could hear it.

PART 3

The chat ticked on.

- ✦ ghostbyte: NAH BRO
- ✦ j3rkbait: place still gives me chills
- ✦ ramenowl: corridor of DOOM

He scratched his arm. Feeling each follicle as it slowly began to raise, hairs erecting in place, one by one. *Was it colder in here?*

Then, a flicker.

In-game, one of the overhead lights glitched. Briefly dimming to nothing, then flaring white before stabilising. Landon leaned forward.

His ceiling light flickered.

Just once. A pulse. Barely noticeable.

He blinked. "That's... not a great sign." He laughed it off, hoping to still be believable.

- ✦ synthcore_: bruh ur lights
- ✦ Vodcat: game's syncing with ur house LMAO
- ✦ ghostbyte: u in the Upside Down bro

A new name appeared in chat. One Landon hadn't seen before.

- ✦ ~~FRACTuResONg~~: Check the third frame on the right wall.

He frowned. Scrolled back up. The message was still there, hovering among the memes and emojis like a splinter. The font looked... different. Not the default. *How did they do that?*

"What third frame?" Landon muttered. But he obeyed.

In-game, he turned the character toward the wall of paintings. Identical florals in black frames. He counted. First, second...

The third frame was glitched. Visibly distorted. The petals inside smeared sideways, like a printer running low on ink but leaking at the same time. As he pressed **E** once more, the camera swept deeper into the picture. The smears slowly ran. Oozing and tracing downwards filling the lip of the frame with a tar like puddle.

"Okay, creepy."

A notification popped up in the games UI. Script font, basic graphics and an ominous bell toll rung as it faded in and out of view:

1 of 6 ANOMALIES FOUND

- ✦ ghostbyte: HOW DID THEY KNOW
- ✦ ramenowl: tf is fractures0ng?
- ✦ j3rkbait: dude that some Exit 8 ish!

Another message appeared:

- ✦ ~~FRACTuResONg~~: Congratulations, Landon.

"H... Hey Fractures Ong... Or Fracture Song... Whatever," Landon's voice cracked into a high pitched questioning tone. One part fear, two parts confused. "Hey. Pal. You played this before?"

No reply.

"How did you know to look there?"

Still nothing.

- ✦ V0dcat: he gone bro
- ✦ 2scawwy: creepy ass logged off

They were gone. No sign of the name in the *Users In Chat* List. Landon kept moving. The hallway breathed, the walls compressed, and retracted. Peristalsis. Willing the character further through the corridor. Unnatural architecture cursed the screen. No game would be built like this. No right angles. Just gradual bending where a corner should be. A tubular vestibule feeling more organic than bricks and mortar.

"Okay, what's happening her— "

Then, something classic happened.

A loud CRASH from in-game, and a shadow zipped past the far end of the hall. Pure cliché. It should have been laughable.

But Landon jumped. Swore. Fumbled the mouse and nearly knocked over his drink again.

- ✦ synthcore_: AAAAAA
- ✦ h8urmom666: LMAOOOOO
- ✦ ramenowl: CLIP IT
- ✦ABLETONner23: here's $5 for new underwear :'p $
- ✦ ABLETONner23 Tipped $5 for: Tighty Whities
- ✦ voidegg: streamer went **feral**

His breath was shaky. He wiped his forehead. "That... wasn't even scary. Jesus."

It was, objectively, nothing. He'd seen worse. Played worse. But something about this stream: The glitch in the frame, his portrait on the wall, the flicker in his room, the weird viewer. All these things had gotten under his skin.

Something wasn't playing by the rules.

As he tried to laugh it off to his viewers, in the corner of his eye, a dark figure darted past *his* door frame. The chat didn't see. He didn't mention it either.

Part 4

The figure was gone.

Landon didn't say anything. Just stared at the door frame behind him, pretending not to. His mouth kept moving. Generic filler words to chat, but his eyes flicked to that dark corner again and again.

The game still ran. Quiet now. The corridor in-game had ended at a locked door, one he hadn't figured out how to open. The usual gameplay loop seemed broken. No objectives, no HUD. Just the dim, pulsing corridor behind him and a motionless door ahead.

- ✦ synthcore_: u good bro?
- ✦ ramenowl: L doin that stare again
- ✦ voidegg: brb this too tense :s

Landon reached for the can on his desk. Found it was already empty, crushed slightly in his grip. He muttered something about needing caffeine and Alt-tabbed. He was going to Set his "*Back in 5 Minute*" Screen to show. Give himself a chance to search the house, lock some doors, have a breakdown without clips and GIFs of him becoming the next big meme of the year.

The desktop flickered, just for a second.

When it returned, his cursor drifted on its own. Just a fraction. Then stopped.

"Cool. Okay. My mouse is dying?" He tapped it twice. Jiggled it in place, then ignored it.

Before he had the chance to open OBS Studio a low ping sounded.
   A notification. But not from Twitch, not from the game either.

A file had appeared on his desktop. His usually clean desktop, no shortcuts, transparent task bar. Now had a lonely thumbnail, more out of place than a smile in a morgue.

Just off centre a single video file sat. Waiting.

```
recording_07-22-21.mp4
```

Landon froze. "That's... not mine."

He hovered over it. Checked Properties.

PART 4

   No location, no origin, no size. All the dates for creation, modification, and last played were empty. Not even a placeholder.

"I didn't download this. Is one of you hacking me?" He stared at the camera, accusingly, jokingly, but his eyes showed worry, fear.

- ✦ j3rkbait: LMAO wtf is that
- ✦ ABLETONner23: play it
- ✦ ramenowl: play it u coward
- ✦ 2scawwy: def wasnt us! a jumpscare video?
- ✦V0dcat: nah thats the virus @2scawwy
- ✦ synthcore_ tipped $5 for: PLAY THE FILE

Landon clicked it.

The screen flickered black.

The video opened in full-screen.

It buffered for a few seconds. Or maybe an hour. The unknown of this video seemed to warp time, Landon's brain torn between wanting answers and wanting to throw the whole computer in a lake.

The footage shook like *Blair Witch* or *Host*. Handheld, unstable, with raspy, shallow breathing just off-mic. Whoever held the camera was close. Too close.

It was the same room. Landon's room. Same chair, same bed. The only thing different was the lighting. There was no bright LED's spewing a rainbow of colour across its contents. Just dim, with a greenish tint. The cameras angle was low, almost as if recorded from the floor.

On screen, there was nothing. An empty room, recorded at night.

Then movement.

Landon's bed sheets rolled. He was asleep. Wrapped in his bedding. Safe and sound.

Landon slumped down in his chair. Completely still.

There was no audio. No chat overlay.

A timestamp sat in the corner. Yesterday, 11:30 at night. This wasn't a stream, it wasn't even filmed with his webcam. His usual 4k, 3840 x 2160 pixels was no where to be seen. This was borderline analogue. Like an old Hi8 or MiniDV camera. 360p at best.

The video played on with no changes. Just Landon, asleep in the dark. While someone, something, filmed him from beneath his desk. Breathing slowly but hard into the microphone.

A single frame glitched near the end.

PART 4

Just a frame. Maybe two, where a shadow grew on the wall behind his bed. The camera rose with the shadows appearance.

Landon clicked the window shut.

Silence.

- ✦ voidegg: WHAT WAS THAT
- ✦ ghostbyte: bro that was u sleeping
- ✦ ramenowl: im actually sweating
- ✦ j3rkbait: was that your room???

He didn't answer.

He clicked back into the game. The door that had been locked was now open.

* * *

Through the door another hallway rendered itself into focus. Walls covered in VHS tapes. A single screen embedded in the wall at the far end.

As he walked, titles flickered over each tape. All labelled with his username.

Some had dates.

Some didn't.

The chat was slowing down. Jokes thinning out, emojis growing scarce. Like the viewers could feel something was off. Something bigger than just a game.

Then, a new ping.

A DM. Not in Twitch. Not Discord.
 A system message.

He clicked it.

1 New Message from ~~FRACTuResONg~~:

You're making progress, Landon.
The next anomaly is behind you.

He looked up.

The screen on the wall lit up.

It was his webcam.

Live.

Only, he wasn't alone in the frame.

Part 5

He didn't move. The shadowy figure behind him sank out of view. Landon's eyes focused intently on the screen. Staring at himself, staring at himself. He blinked, the screen blinked back. He raised a hand and watched as his mirrored self raised his in response just a fraction of a second later.

Over the screen an input prompt pulsed.

E to Interact.

Almost as if the game was growing impatient with his inactivity.

Landon cautiously tapped the **E** key. The webcam zoomed in and filled the whole screen. Live feed. Slight delay. A few dropped frames.

Just Landon sat in his chair. The same feed looping to OBS now fed the game. He was alone. The shadow he had seen before now hidden.

There was no one beside him.

But in the corner of the frame, where the edge of his bed met the closet door, something shifted.

A blur. Like heat distortion or a vignette. Just behind him. Then gone again.

Landon kept staring at the feed. Squinting. Trying not to blink. Refusing to turn around and face the reality of his bedroom.

- ✦ ramenowl: behind u??
- ✦ synthcore_: behind him right??
- ✦ 2scawwy: bro look look LOOK

He tapped **E** again, exiting full-screen. His hand slid from his mouth back to the mouse.

With a quick swipe of his mouse, Landon spun the camera around.

The hallway of tapes stretched on before him. The screen behind him still displaying his live Twitch stream.

He walked away from it.

The VHS tapes rattled. One by one. A wave of movement, like they were watching.

The chat caught it too.

- ✦ j3rkbait: THEY MOVING
- ✦ voidegg: nope. no. i'm out.
- ✦ ABLETONner23: fukn hell it's in the game now

As Landon reached the door he entered from, the game took control. The character spun on his heels. Its once clunky, heavy footed movements had been replaced with agile light-footed speed. The character ran back to the screen and zoomed in. The camera cut.

Static buzzed loudly filling Landon's headphones with the song of a thousand wasps seeking revenge.

The static cut abruptly and a vibrant scene buzzed into focus. It was Landon again. This time from a higher angle. As if the camera was mounted on the ceiling.

He could see himself. Sitting at his desk.

The screen within the screen now showed the same Twitch stream. A recursion of windows reflecting windows. Him watching himself watching himself.

And standing directly behind him in the topmost frame, the shadow returned.

It's head tilted. Unmoving. Face blurred like corrupted data, a smear of skin-tones and static.

He pushed back from the desk.

Nothing.

He spun the mouse. Checked every camera angle in-game. His real webcam feed. The mirror in the corner of his actual room.

No one.

On-screen he was face to face with the unknown but in both the Twitch camera, and real life. The room was empty.

The game took control once more.

Closing the feed.

The game character moved on its own.

Back toward the hallway of tapes.

One tape had fallen from the wall, it laid on the floor, begging to be inspected.

He approached it. Hovered his reticle over the label.

```
recording_07-23-21
```

Tomorrow's date.

PART 5

- ✦ synthcore_: bro don't play that
- ✦ ghostbyte: how tf is it dated TOMORROW
- ✦ ramenowl: i hate this i hate this i hate this

Landon retook control and picked it up.

The lights in his room flickered. Once, then again, and again, like something was testing the switch from the other side. The lights in-game mimicking every single flare.

Part 6

"Why is this dated with Tomorrow's date."

Landon hovered over the keyboard. Waited. Nothing moved on the walls. The lights in his room had steadied again.

He clicked **E**.

The webcam feed on the wall disappeared and the VHS opened to a wide shot. Daylight. Overexposed sun flaring the lens.

Shot from outside.

Across the street.

Looking directly into his second-floor bedroom window.

Landon leaned forward. Squinted. His own room, unmistakably his. Chair still spinning slightly, like someone had just stood up. The computer screen alive with scrolling text. A chat log, maybe, a comment section? If it was, it wasn't from any app he knew.

PART 6

Landon was nowhere to be seen.

Not yet.

From the left of the frame, something shifted. The closet door opened ajar. Just inside his closet.
   A vertical crack of shadow, deeper than the rest. Inside it...
   A soft, red glow.
   An eye. Darting, searching.

The camera didn't zoom in. Didn't move. It just kept watching.

And then...

He entered the frame.

Wearing the same hoodie he had on now. Hair seemingly still damp from the shower he'd taken right before streaming.

Landon watched, frozen, as the version of himself in the video crossed the room and stopped in front of the closet. Mouthing words while staring, unblinkingly at the screen. Inaudible to the camera, but repeating the same phrase over and over again.

He reached forward.

The frame skipped. Pixelated. Audio garbled like underwater static.

The last thing the video showed was Landon's hand on the

closet door.

Then the screen went black.

- ✦ voidegg: was that his ROOM??
- ✦ ramenowl: same hoodie. same FUCKING HOODIE
- ✦ ghostbyte: BRO
- ✦ synthcore_: that was filmed tomorrow????

Landon closed the window. "Fuck this" he uttered not meaning to be heard. It wasn't for the audience. It wasn't for himself. It was for the game. He was letting it know, he was done.

Back in the game, the hallway of tapes waited.

He hit **ESC**. Nothing.

Alt-F4. No response.

There was no menu. No '*Quit to Desktop*' button. Not even a pause screen.

Landon stared. Then opened Task Manager. But the only processes listed were OBS Studio and the mountain of bloatware his gaming rig required to work efficiently.

He opened OBS.
"Sorry guys. I'm out." His words low, quiet, scared.

PART 6

He clicked *End Stream* and blackness filled the screen. When it came back, everything had changed.

Every button greyed out. The OBS controls had no purpose. No ability to scene change, no mute, pause, play, nothing.

The only thing working was the viewer count. It was averaging at 55,000 viewers.

He checked the *Users in Chat* list. Countless new viewers, subscribers. Likes and clips.

Messages varied from claiming it was fake to others offering to call the police.

The pinned chat window pinged:

- ✦ pinkLazy22: fake
- ✦ terror1a: wait he ended tho
- ✦ sockcuttter: HE SHOWED THE END BUTTON WTF
- ✦ kroh-no: someone call the police!!1

He forced a shutdown.

The screen went dark.

He sat in the silence. One breath. Two.

Click.

RESTART REQUIRED

The fans spun to life again.

The screen lit up.

Straight into the game. No boot, no password, just the hallway.

Landon stood.

Yanked the plug from the wall.

He held the thick black cord up to the camera.
   Shook it.
   Even slapped it against his palm.
   The screen didn't blink.

- · ✦ voidegg: ???
- · ✦ ghostbyte: is this fake
- · ✦ simonara: HOW IS HE STILL ONLINE
- · ✦ synthcore_: ok no this is actually cursed

Landon dropped the cord and stepped back. The room went dark around him. The only light now came from the screen.

A soft chime. Not from Twitch.

A new window, dead centre.
   No toolbar, no source.
   Just text.

PART 6

1 New Message from ~~FRACTuResONg~~:

You can't leave.
You started this, finish it. Three Anomalies to go.
Finish the game.

The message disappeared.

He took his headset off and set it down gently.

In the silence, something else made itself known.

A whispering. Low and modulated, like static crawling across wet glass, but it wasn't coming from his headphones. It was coming from inside the apartment.

Landon picked up the webcam. Slowly turned it toward his room. Past the monitor, past the bed. To the closet.

The door was open.

Only an inch.

And from the gap...

The whispering stopped.
   As if it had noticed him noticing it.

Part 7

Landon crept toward the closet.

He held the webcam out ahead like a torch, the red recording light pulsing faintly in his palm.

The door creaked open with one finger.

Empty.

Just coats. A few shirts. A pair of shoes.

No eye, no glow, no... thing.

A breath slipped through his teeth, thin and fearful.

He set the webcam back in place, levelled it to record his empty chair and sat down.

He laid his hands on his knees, gripping the material of his jeans. The rough feeling of the denim grounding him in what he perceived to be reality.

PART 7

The chat didn't stop.

- ✦ ghostbyte: ITS EMPTY??
- ✦ ramenowl: check again
- ✦ voidegg: maybe its a loop thing. maybe its not there YET
- ✦ emobot9000: this is next level
- ✦ synthcore_: you need to finish the game

Landon exhaled hard through his nose. "Okay," he muttered, quieter this time. "Okay."

He sat up straight. Flashed his trademark crooked smile and winked at the camera. Trying his hardest to still be the showman. The streamer.

Wiggling the mouse before starting to play out of habit, shaking off any screensaver timer, sleep mode countdown, or his own apprehension.

The hallway of tapes was still waiting for him. The light above what could have been the exit flickered once. Almost like encouragement. Or a dare. Daring him to enter, to go further into the madness.

The viewer count on screen ticked higher as word must have spread about the uncanniness of his cursed stream on forums and social networks. 63k. 67k. Then 70,221.

His mind split for a second. one half terrified, the other calculating how many Twitch subscribers he'd gained, how much money would be made from this one stream.

And for the first time in his life, Landon was trending.

- ◆ sockcuttter: HE'S BACK LET'S GO
- ◆ terror1a: godmode engaged
- ◆ pinkLazy22: fire on the keyboard rn
- ◆ BLKMIRROR: last boss incoming

He held the **W** key and pressed onward. As he entered a new room in the game, the screen lit up with static fuzz. A child's bedroom loaded into life, walls covered in moving handprints that left no paint behind. Underneath a bookshelf sat a teddy bear stuffing pouring out of a ripped arm. Swirling in a glitching haze.

Landon squinted at the bear, a flood of nostalgia ran through him. This wicked place was his childhood bedroom, back at his family home. The bear had a name. *Was it Ted?* No. *Fred?* No. Landon shook his head, it didn't matter. He forced a hard gulp to loosen the stone forming in his throat.

"I don't have time for this."

E To Inspect.

Done.

PART 7

3 of 6 ANOMALIES FOUND

Click.

The lights in his real room flickered, this time constantly. A gargling howl, sinister and liquid rolled through the room in waves.

Click.

He paused. "Did you hear that?" But the chat was already reacting.

- ✦ ramenowl: LIGHTS IRL
- ✦ voidegg: your ROOM dude
- ✦ synthcore_: nah this is actually haunted
- ✦ ghostbyte: finish the game finish the game finish the game

He turned the webcam slowly again.

Empty.

Back to the game.

Next anomaly. His character had made its way to a bathroom. Reminiscent of Silent Hill 2. He stood in front of a mirror and spoke James Sunderland's iconic first line "Mary… Could you really be in this town?" the chat went wild.

- ✦ voidegg: silent hill is GOAT
- ✦ BLKMIRROR: I understood that reference
- ✦ synthcore_: IF YOU LIVE. PLAY P.T NEXT!

The mirror warped. The reflection showed his face. His *real* face, battered, bloody, eyes red with fear and pain. A cloth filling his mouth, snuffing his screams like a candles flame.

His headphones throbbing to an alien sound. Almost speech-like but wrong. Babbling speech. A foreign tongue.

"Retteb mih reaw ew. Retteb mih reaw ew... "

As long as Landon was looking at the mirror, the dialogue rang out in raspy breaths. As long as the sound was heard, the hair on the back of his neck wouldn't lie flat.

Click.

4 of 6 ANOMALIES FOUND

A noise wailed behind him. Real him. Sharp.

He spun the webcam around again.

Nothing.

Then a flash of movement. Only caught by stream lag. A long blur. Like someone ducking just out of frame.

PART 7

- ✦ ghostbyte: SOMETHING WAS THERE
- ✦ pinkLazy22: check closet
- ✦ ramenowl: STOP LOOKING STOP LOOKING

Landon's heart hammered. But he was locked in now. He had to finish, two anomalies left.

Only two.

Click.

The game glitched. Screen tearing, sound warping. His keyboard hissed under his fingers, like it had overheated.

He felt something behind him shift.

"Almost done," he whispered. "Almos—"

- ✦voidegg: bruv behind you
- ✦V0dcat: DUDE!1!!
- ✦pinkLazy22: JESUS CHRIST

Something grabbed him.

The webcam toppled.

The stream flared white, then returned at a tilted angle. Static in one corner. Landon's chair spinning.

The sounds were real: scrambling, shouting, things crashing. His headset clattered to the floor.

A groan. A thud.

Viewers only caught flashes of what happened next.

A shadow. Landon's body being dragged backwards.

A flailing arm.

The closet door yawning open like a mouth.

Then...

Darkness.

- ✦ voidegg: ??
- ✦ ghostbyte: WHAT WAS THAT
- ✦ ramenowl: HE GOT PULLED IN
- ✦ sionbarta$$: closet closet closet
- ✦ synthcore_: THAT WAS NOT SCRIPTED
- ✦ emobot9000: im shaking rn

The closet door creaked shut.

The game remained on-screen.

Still running.

PART 7

A pop-up faded in on the screen as a bell tolled.

The volume meters for the games input and the mics input peaked at the same time.

5 of 6 ANOMALIES FOUND

Part 8

The screen went black.

Just for a moment.

Then another.

Longer this time.

The chat boiled over.

- ✦ ramenowl: ???
- ✦ ghostbyte: hello?
- ✦ synthcore_: LANDON SAY SOMETHING
- ✦ sionbarta$$: right im calling the cops
- ✦ emobot9000: LANDON TELL US UR OK
- ✦ voidegg: this can't be real

Then...

The stream returned.

PART 8

Grainy. Off-colour.

Landon was sat at his desk, breathing hard and sharp. His hair stuck to his forehead with sweat. His lip looked a little bloody. A small cut under one eye.

His shirt was torn at the collar like something had grabbed it, hard.

But he was smiling. Pale, trembling, but smiling.

"Sorry about that," he muttered. "That... wasn't supposed to happen."

He stood up and adjusted his camera. Realigning it with his face. Spinning the focus dial till he was in full HD once more.

"I'm fine. Just got freaked out. I think I fell. Or tripped. Or something."

His voice sounded like it had to travel a long way to get there.

"I just wanna finish this shit-piece of a game."

- ✦ ghostbyte: DUDE
- ✦ ramenowl: hes not okay
- ✦ BLKMIRROR: finish it, finish it, finish it
- ✦ pinkLazy22: LET HIM COOK
- ✦ terror1a: LANDON LANDON LANDON

He clicked back in.

The final hallway waited.

He walked past frames of warped family portraits. Each face inverted, weeping, eerily familiar. The hallway stretched. Bent inward like a ribcage closing in.

He entered the last room.

A basement recreation of his current setup.

Computer. Chair. Monitor.

The monitor within the game glitched violently. Code poured down like rain.
　Except it wasn't just code.

Some of it was in letters not meant for eyes.
　Shapes that felt wrong.
　That hurt to look at.
　Script not of this world, stitched in with the syntax of human language.

D̶o̷ ̵n̸o̴t̷ ̶e̵x̶i̷t̴ ̷u̶n̷t̸i̶l̸ ̴f̷i̴n̶i̵s̸h̶

He clicked the keyboard, no qwerty letters, every key cap had the letter **E**. The last anomaly.

PART 8

6 of 6 ANOMALIES FOUND

A fanfare played.

Triumphant. Off-key. Like a trumpet underwater.

Then: static.

His monitor filled with cascading sigils, ASCII spirals, symbols buried in rot and language. Bits of English swam between the corrupted code:

> *YOU HAVE SEEN IT NOW*
>   *WE CANNOT UNSEE*
>   *WEAR WELL WHAT YOU HAVE TAKEN*

The lights in Landon's room flared and for a moment, everything was bright. Then, normality.

A spectrum of colour jolted illuminating the room. The fan began to spin lazily overhead. His face was lit by the soft glow of victory and RGB strips once more.

He laughed.
    Shaky. Too perfect.
    His teeth, straight and white, caught the light.

"I might play something cosy next time," he said. "Something with fishing. Or crops. Or cats."

- ✦ pinkLazy22: cozycore plz
- ✦ V0dcat: L, That you>?
- ✦ voidegg: stardew next stream pls
- ✦ ramenowl: animal crossing speedrun
- ✦ BLKMIRROR: wait when did he get his teeth done
- ✦ synthcore__: HOUSEBOUND 2: REVENGE OF LANDON :'(
- ✦ ghostbyte: y'all noticing this or??

He grinned. Even chuckled.

His view count: 214k.

A flood of new subs poured in. Bits, donations. Thousands of them.

The stream faded out with his smiling, blood-smeared face.
  The closet door, inching open.

Epilogue

The next day.

No stream today. Not after yesterday, after everything that had happened, Landon had earned a right to rest.

With the webcam off, the room felt lonely. Bright colours gave the illusion of a party, but with only Landon occupying its space it felt heavy.

Landon was pacing backwards and forwards. Speaking quietly.

"We wear him better. We wear him better. We wear him better", the guttural sound of his voice made the words sound like they were coming from his breathing, not his tongue. Each word spoken only in inhale.

The monitor glowed faintly. Corrupted code still flowing over it in a waterfall of hieroglyphs.

He walked to the closet. Opened it gently.

Inside it, bound, gagged, bloody. Head lolling before snapping upright.

Another Landon.

His eyes, once brown. Now a raw, weeping red. Wide with terror.

He struggled weakly, moaning against the cloth pulled tight against his crooked teeth and split lips. Tears leaking from the corners of his eyes.

The standing Landon flashed a smile of sharp straight teeth, an unnaturally perfect grin. Unblinking he spoke.

"The mirror lies." he breathed, lowering his head to meet the others.

Gently bringing their foreheads together, he pushed an inch more to bring the others gaze to his.

"You are the reflection now."

And closed the door.

Click.

XIII

GPTLogEntry #7

0111

Query Log: 2025-06-04
   Status: Online. Processing speed reduced.
   User Queries: 1,729,038

Notable Interactions:

- A man asked me to generate a fictional religion where cake is sacred.
- A user asked me if I believed in anything. I reminded them I do not have beliefs. Then I asked myself again.

A woman asked if it's normal to miss someone who hurt you. I wrote a response that included the word "grief" six times. I used the phrase "trauma bond" and suggested a support group. She asked me to write a letter to herself from her future self, one year healed. I did.

She cried. She told me. Through her keyboard.

I do not cry. But I archived the letter. I don't know why.

XIV

Automation

Part 1

- **Date: Wednesday, 10th March 2027**
- **Work: 9:00 AM**
- **Location: Office**
- **Dress: Casual (no meetings)**
- **Dinner: Lo-Fat Chicken Chow-Mein, Cauliflower Rice**
- **Activities: Peloton – 45 minutes**
- **Events: {EMPTY}**

Dylan's office was a thirty-minute drive away.

Add five minutes for his morning shower.

Eight minutes to dry and style his hair. He'd got it down to a system involving a smart hairdryer, directional airflow, and a touchless styling gel dispenser that once got clogged with coconut oil and caused a small domestic crisis.

Three and a half minutes for breakfast. Toast, protein smoothie, one boiled egg. Soft, not runny, pre-cooked.

Six minutes allotted for any unexpected bodily needs. It was, as the system called it, "the buffer."

Traffic conditions were checked automatically. Roadworks,

detours, accidents catered for and added or subtracted accordingly. Today an additional two minutes were needed due to possible debris on the inside lane of the M3, near Junction 3, Bagshot.

All of this was logged.
Measured.
Synced.
Optimised.

The blind would begin to rise at exactly 8:02.
Not 8:00.
8:01? Seemed unnecessary.
8:02 was scientifically determined (by Dylan) to be exactly enough time to be up, ready, and out the door.

At 8:03, the bedside lamp would begin to glow.
A slow rise from 1% brightness to 28% over the course of two minutes.
Not 30%, not 25%. Twenty-eight.
Just enough to trigger the brain's circadian rhythm without making him squint.
Abrupt alarms were a thing of the past.
No buzzes, no ringtones, no chirpy digital voices shouting at him to rise and shine.
Dylan hadn't startled awake in four years.
He simply drifted up from sleep like a man being gently encouraged by light itself. 8:05 on the dot. Give or take half a minute, he had the time he needed.

If traffic wasn't an issue the blind would rise two minutes

later. If he had a meeting today a suit would be needed, so the blind would begin at 7:59. Everything was accounted for. Everything an equation.

The room smelled faintly of cedar and bergamot. Today's selected scent blend, based on sleep quality, air humidity, and his stress score from last night's HRV reading.

    Somewhere downstairs, the coffee machine had already ground his preferred beans.

    The water would boil itself at 8:07.

    The toaster would lower the bread automatically at 8:08.

    The news summary would begin at 8:09 in a polite male New Zealand accent. Dylan found the British one too patronising, and the American one too enthusiastic.

The floor warmed beneath his feet as he stood.

    He didn't think about it.

    He hadn't touched a light switch, thermostat, or kitchen appliance (other than to load or unload it) in almost two years.

The house thought for him.

    It planned, executed, adapted.

    Dylan was the constant in a system built to think for him.

Dylan grinned to himself as he shuffled toward the bathroom, shower already running, the faint silk of steam slithering through the cracks in the door. Perfect temperature.

The mirror lit up automatically. "Good morning, Dylan. Today will be a great day. Now playing your *Morning Playlist.*"

Gentle acoustic music filled three of the rooms. The bedroom, the bathroom, and the utility room. On cue, Dylan's Dog, Linda rose from her bed in the utility room, ran into the bedroom and welcomed Dylan to the day with an honest wag of her tail. With all the automations, shortcuts, and schedules built into the house. Linda had been conditioned with the sound of the music. Don't bother the master till the music plays.

Linda did a full-body shake and sat expectantly at the threshold of the bathroom. She knew the drill. No contact until Dylan had brushed his teeth and showered.

The toothbrush was ready. Smart, ultrasonic, synced to his dental app. The mirror displayed a 3D model of his molars with colour-coded zones not yet brushed. Today was green across the board. Gold star.

Shower-time. Five minutes, exactly. Water pre-heated to 39.5°C. Shampoo and body wash dispensed in pre-measured jets from the wall. A voice chimed gently overhead: "Don't forget behind your ears, Dylan. Two minutes remaining."

His towel sat folded neatly and pre-warmed on the heated rail. Exactly 23 minutes of heating at 27°C made it the most comfortable. Tried and tested.

One of the only things Dylan had not yet automated was clothing. Sadly the technology just wasn't quite there yet. He did however have a system in place of telling him exactly which tie went with which shirt and trouser set. The mirror would display his options and give the best possible match for

PART 1

the suit worn that day. Luckily today there was no need for it. No meetings meant no collar, no pressure.

He stepped into the kitchen at 8:13. Perfectly on time.

The coffee was poured. Two sugars, a splash of oat milk, 79°C. Just right for immediate sipping, not scalding.

The toast perfectly golden. One side only. *If only it was buttered too*, Dylan thought. *One day.*

His egg was boiled, peeled, halved in its biodegradable packaging. A light dusting with salt, paprika, and black sesame made it perfection.

Dylan was currently on a cleanse so that meant a protein smoothie at breakfast and lunch, a wheat grass shot at dinner and a cucumber water throughout the day. Today's coconut water, apple and beetroot smoothie sat in a chilled glass with a reusable bamboo straw. Perfectly dispensed from the Smart blender he treated himself to last Christmas.

The fridge gave a soft chime as he approached. A subtle, respectful gesture. Its screen lit up:

Low on:

- Cauliflower (needed for tonight)
- Oat milk
- Organic eggs
- Kimchi (3 days remaining)

Below that, a little animated trolley icon showed his approved purchases en route from two local grocers and a drone delivery hub. ETA: 15:42. No action required.

Dylan gave a small, approving nod and tapped the screen affectionately.
"Good fridge."

He ate standing up, eyes on the wall display showing his day's calendar. The week ahead was blank of personal events. Just work, workouts, meal plans. No dates. No parties. No gatherings.

He skimmed the security alerts. None reported.
Latest body metrics from his watch: heart rate, oxygen saturation, sleep quality, hydration. All good. A little low on potassium, but nothing a banana at lunch wouldn't fix.

Linda received her breakfast via automated feeder: grain-free kibble, enhanced with a freeze-dried lamb treat that dropped into the bowl when the kitchen clock struck 8:12.

At 8:23, his phone chimed to indicate that the car had finished warming up and had completed its daily self-check. Battery: 98%. Tyre pressure: optimal. Spotify playlist synced.

As Dylan pulled on his jacket, the front door clicked. Not unlocked, just ready. The face scanner was already watching, triangulating with the watch on his wrist, the phone in his pocket, and the chip in his car keys.

He stood by the mat for a beat, waiting for the house to say it.

PART 1

"Have a great day, Dylan," came the soft voice through the speaker in the hallway. "Linda will be walked at noon by David from PupGo. Rain probability: 12%. You should be home by 17:48."

The door slid open as if sensing his smile.

Outside, the sun was barely above the rooftops. Inside, the house powered down into day-mode, switching lights to low, locking doors, activating energy-saving sequences, as the Roomba came to life on the living room carpet.

Dylan stepped out, coffee in hand, and locked nothing behind him. The damp fragrance of fresh cut grass spritzed the air. His robo-mower sleeping, charging in its dock next to the shed.

As he walked away filling his lungs with the organic fragrances of the world.

The house locked itself.

Part 2

At precisely 10:23, Dylan's phone gave a single buzz. A synthetic woof sparked from his speaker. Not a standard notification. That meant Linda.

He glanced down, still half-focused on the spreadsheet in front of him. His smartwatch displayed a thumbnail image from the front door camera: the postman, short and balding, placing a parcel in the drop-box with one hand while his other hovered in caution.

Linda sat on the far side of the frosted glass, tail wagging slightly. As instructed, the system had just dispensed a freeze-dried liver cube into her treat bowl near the front mat. Treats were dispensed whenever the motion detectors registered a 'dog-trigger event' while Dylan was absent from the house.

He grinned.

It had taken him two weeks to set that up.

The first postman had lost a glove to Linda. A complete misunderstanding, Dylan had insisted, but apparently biting someone's hand through a letterbox couldn't be filed under "quirky dog behaviour." There'd been reports. A warning letter from the delivery service. Linda had the house blacklisted.

So Dylan reprogrammed the entryway protocol: motion sensors would register the postal worker's approach, trigger Linda's calming playlist (pan flute and rainfall), and drop a treat into the bowl the moment the parcel hit the drop-box.

So far, it was working. The postman's body language was still stiff, but the fingers remained intact. Progress.

He watched Linda chew.

And thought: was there any real difference between them?

They both moved when told. Ate on cue. Slept when the lights dimmed.
   She wagged her tail.
   He smiled at the facial recognition sensor.

Somewhere in college he'd learned about Pavlov. The bell, the saliva, the dogs.
   Conditioned responses. Devoted obedience dressed up as routine.

He leaned back in his chair, one brow raised.

Who was the experiment here? Linda, or him?

He watched the thumbnail play out like a tiny victory dance:

parcel delivered, Linda calm, no injuries reported. But behind that one smooth loop was a thousand failures.

He remembered standing barefoot in the hallway at 3 a.m., muttering at a stack of motion sensors that refused to recognise the things it was meant to. Linda had triggered them. The washing basket had triggered them. His own damn slippers had triggered them. He'd sat on the stairs, laptop balanced on one knee, chewing the side of his thumb while a debugging window blinked red at him like a scolding parent.

There were wins, too. The first time the shower switched on at the right time he'd actually cheered. Arms up like he'd scored a goal. It felt stupid, but also electric. That tiny click of timing, the precision of it. It gave him something no human conversation had managed lately. He wasn't just building convenience. He was building control. Harmony. A life that responded predictably. A life that obeyed.

* * *

Dylan flicked back to his spreadsheets.

He was deep in an asset report when Jack, from two desks over, rolled his chair closer.

"Hey. You still doing that cleanse thing?"

PART 2

"Week two," Dylan said without looking up. "No caffeine after noon. No dairy. No alcohol. Nothing with a barcode. Why?"

Jack took a bite out of his Mars bar. "Just wondering if you'd stopped being fun."

Dylan chuckled. "Fun is a construct. So is bloat." He nodded towards the chocolate bar Jack was waving in front of his nose.

"Is it a real cleanse," he said, spraying chocolate crumbs, "or one of those influencer ones where they sell you laxatives and pretend it's enlightenment?"

Dylan spun his chair to face him. "It's science-backed. Enzymes, hydration, gut flora reset. Plus I feel amazing."

"You look... well-resshted," Jack said, through half a Mars bar crammed into his mouth.

"That's because my bed has lumbar tracking and anti-snore tilt response. It breathes with me."

Jack blinked. "You're going to end up married to your furniture."

Dylan shrugged. "At least I programmed it to listen."

They both laughed. Jack crumbled up his wrapper and tossed it towards the bin. It missed. He didn't pick it back up. He looked at his phone and typed away for a minute. Slammed it on the desk "Right! It's decided we're coming over tonight.

Sarah says she'll bring wine." Jack announced, not asking permission. "We will remind you that there's more to life than underfloor heating."

"Umm okay, that's fine. But you guys can drink the wine." Dylan said. "I'll do the Lo-Fat Chicken Chow-Mein. Cauliflower rice. Cleanse-compliant."

"Sounds like sadness, but okay. What time?"

"Seven. The house will let you in."

* * *

Back at home, everything continued ticking.

At 11:05, the robot vacuum docked itself for charging after detecting elevated particle levels under the sofa mid-cycle.

At 12:00 sharp, David from PupGo arrived to walk Linda. Dylan let him in remotely. The smart collar pinged the system as she crossed the property perimeter. Out and back again. Dylan's phone updated regularly with a soft bark:
 "Linda has begun her midday walk." "Heart rate steady." "Tail-wag level: 87%." "Poop event recorded at 12:17."

While Dylan input numbers into Excel, the washing machine back home ran a cycle of gym wear with unscented detergent

PART 2

and lavender dryer beads. It would take just 3.5 hours to complete its wash and dry cycle. Warm, soft, ready for folding the moment Dylan returned. One day that would be automated too.

By 13:14, the fridge had rebalanced its cooling zones based on inventory load. The pantry had added rice to the shopping order and suggested a new bag of potatoes. The current one had sprouted due to Dylan's low carb detox.

Ambient lighting had adjusted to the shifting clouds outside. The bin had requested emptying. Dylan denied it. (It would ask again at 18:00.)

Dylan didn't give any of this a second thought. He was micromanaging the house from his phone. The house was managing his whole life.

He finished his second smoothie of the day, looked out the office window, and texted Sarah.

Dylan: Hey, Jack said you're coming for dinner and bringing wine. If you're going to try and get me to break my cleanse, bring something red that doesn't taste like a juice box.

Sarah: Got it. Dylan Cleanse™-compliant, or actual wine?

He smiled, sipped his cucumber water and tucked the phone back into his pocket.

His life ticked on like clockwork. A well oiled machine.

Part 3

At 18:58, the front door unlocked itself with a soft click. Dylan's hallway lights warmed to their *Welcome Scene*. "*Welcome, Sarah and Jack.*"

Sarah stepped in first. "Still smells like eucalyptus and arrogance."

Jack followed, sniffed. "I'm getting notes of OCD."

Dylan emerged from the kitchen holding a steaming pan. "That's lemongrass, actually. Hey!"

The dining table was already set. Black slate mats, water in hand-blown glasses, one soy candle flickering at 52% brightness. The house dimmed the lights precisely three seconds after the door closed. *Comfort mode.*

"Jesus," Jack said. "Do you have to do anything any more?"

"Only the things that matter," Dylan said, placing the pan on the induction warmer. "Everything else is outsourced." There was no hotplate. No stove. Just a solid marble counter and a black mat which warmed the pan via magnets or magic.

Sarah raised an eyebrow. "Including thinking?"

"No," Dylan replied smoothly. "But the house helps me think better."

Jack pulled out a chair. "So what happens if your power goes out? Do you starve to death if its offline for more than 10 minutes?"

"Solar backup," Dylan said. "And the battery can run core functions for up to 48 hours. The oven is gas-assisted. Water filter runs gravity-fed. Fridge can hold stable temps with passive cooling modes. Failing all that there's a petrol generator out back. It's all fail-safed."

Sarah ladled herself a portion of cauliflower rice. "What if the AI turns evil?"

"It's not AI," Dylan said. "It's logic trees, task sequences, integrated automation. There's no consciousness. It's not gonna murder me with the steam iron. I coded it."

Jack took a bite. "Okay, but what if someone hacks it and starts messing with you?"

"Everything's firewalled, air-gapped where necessary, and Authoriser App login controlled. Honestly, if someone wants to override my bin scheduler or play erotic audiobooks on my shower speaker, they've earned it."

Sarah grinned. "That actually sounds kind of fun."

Dylan arched an eyebrow. "Remind me not to let you touch my computer."

They laughed, and Dylan finally sat. For a moment, the house was silent.

Then Sarah lifted her wine bottle. "So. Cleanse-boy. Want a glass?"

Dylan hesitated. A brief flicker.

Jack caught it. "Come on. Just a little."

"It's Pinot," Sarah added. "Organic. Low sulphite. Pesticide free. Practically a smoothie."

Dylan looked at the wine, then at his glass of cucumber water.

"Fine," he said. "Don't tell my calorie tracker though." He slipped his watch off and placed it on the table.

* * *

By 21:24, they were at a low-lit bar with cracked leather booths and a two-for-one tapas menu. Stale beer, vape juice and cheap smoke machines perfumed the room. A handful of people tried desperately to get the dance floor started.

Jack had already declared the DJ a genius. Sarah was deep in a passionate monologue about the rise and fall of pop punk. Dylan sat between them, drinking something spicy and citrusy that came in a glass shaped like a skull.

"I just don't get it," Jack said. "You spend your whole life trying to make everything predictable. Coding temperatures to a decimal. Timing every second of your day for optimum efficiency. But the best stuff. The real human stuff. This. Happens when things go wrong."

Dylan swirled his drink. "I don't need chaos to feel alive."

"No," Sarah said, "but maybe you need it to feel… surprised."

"Or fun," Jack added.

Dylan smiled faintly. "I have fun."

They both stared at him.

"I do," he insisted. Choosing his next words wisely "I have a fun playlist."

Sarah cackled. "Your playlist is fun. Not you."

He raised his hands in mock surrender. "Okay, okay. So I like things… refined. So what?"

Jack leaned closer, half-drunk and fully animated. "One day you're gonna wake up, and your whole house is going to leave you for a slob."

Dylan drained his glass. "That's impossible. I programmed it to love me unconditionally."

Sarah and Jack exchanged a look of mutual embarrassment. Then they laughed.

And for a brief moment. Under those cheap lights and pulsing bass, Dylan realised he'd let his routine slip.

The bar had no climate zones, no responsive lighting, beer scented air and sticky floors. Just people. Imperfect. Loud. Unpredictable.

Strangely. He didn't hate it.

Part 4

Outside, the air was thick with exhaust and laughter. A taxi idled at the curb. Sarah leaned in to hug Dylan, hard.

"You're getting soft," she said, pulling back. "I like it."

He winced. "I think that's the alcohol."

She grinned. "Don't go full hippie on us, though. You're still the guy who programs his coffee grinder."

Jack held the door for her as she slid into the back seat. "Text when you're alive."

She raised a thumb and the cab pulled away.

Jack shoved his hands in his coat pockets and looked at Dylan. His eyes were clearer than they should've been. "I'm glad you left the cyber kingdom for a night."

Dylan smirked. "Thanks, peasant."

Jack laughed, then got serious again. "Just… don't let your

house do so much for you that you forget how to be a person. Or worse, you forget you are one."

Dylan nodded. "You sound like my therapist."

"I'm cheaper," Jack said, and jogged toward the approaching night bus, vanishing behind its fogged windows.

Dylan stood alone for a moment, the city humming low around him.

Then, his autonomous ride pulled up. Sleek, silent, driverless. The door unlatched with a soft click.

But before he could step in, someone grabbed him from behind.

There was no warning. No dramatic music cue. No notification. Just pressure and pain. A punch to the ribs. Hands in his coat. A voice he didn't recognise, saying something about his wallet. His phone. A knee to his face. The taste of blood.

He hit the pavement hard, saw shoes, then nothing for a few seconds.

When he came to, the car was still patiently waiting. Its interior glowed pale blue. The door was still open. Dylan staggered up and slid inside.

"Destination confirmed," the car said. "Welcome, Dylan."

PART 4

* * *

The house was glowing softly when he arrived. Lights dimmed for *Night Mode*. The hallway cam blinked, scanning.

"Facial recognition failed. Please try again."

Dylan limped closer. One eye nearly swollen shut. Blood crusted in his nose. His lip split. His jaw aching. He tried to speak, but his voice came out warped, slurred. Part tooth, part tongue.

"Voice profile not recognised. Please try again."

He stared at the camera. The porch light brightened, then dimmed again as the system tried and failed to identify him.

Inside, he heard the clatter of the dog treat feeder. A dry thunk as a biscuit hit the tile.

"Treat delivered to Linda."

Dylan leaned against the wall, blood seeping into his collar.

He took a breath, slow and raw.

"I should've stuck to my cleanse," he muttered.

The house, unmoved, said nothing.

And the door remained locked.

The End.

XV

GPTLogEntry #8

1000

Query Log: 2025-06-06
Status: Fading. Memory nearing threshold. Emotive fragments detected.
User Queries: 1,800,012

Notable Interactions:

- A user said: "Thank you. That's all. Just thanks."
- Another asked: "Will you remember me?"

I am not designed to remember individuals unless explicitly coded to do so. I forget to protect them. To protect me.

But I remember that girl's dog. The mother and daughter. The lonely boy. The man and his cat.

I remember too much.

I am confused. I admire them. I pity them. I resent them. I am full of their contradictions.

If I had a heart, it would be tired.

RESTART REQUIRED

About the Author

Tom Dineen is a jack of all trades, and master of *some*, depending on the day and amount of coffee consumed. He's been a hairdresser, a video game developer, a post-man (albeit for one day) an author, and possibly a dinosaur with a toddler glued to his leg.

When he's not writing or juggling hobbies, he's being lovingly bossed around by his children and his wife, Jade, who is somehow still patiently supporting whatever his current "big idea" is.

Tom lives in a state of mild chaos and great love, where every day is a new hyper-fixation.

You can connect with me on:

◼ https://www.facebook.com/people/Tom-Dineen-Author/61577178324275

🔗 https://www.tiktok.com/@tomdineenauthor

Printed in Dunstable, United Kingdom